"Why were you in such a hurry?"

The question sent a wave of fear rushing through her as she recalled what had occurred before she ran into the street. A crowd had gathered. She scanned the group but didn't see a familiar face. But how could she tell who he was? In the two years she'd endured the terror of a stalker, she'd never seen his face.

How could he be alive? And if he was, how had he found her now?

"Ma'am..." The deputy's voice interrupted her thoughts. "Did something happen that frightened you? Is that why you ran in front of my car?"

Cheyenne tried to speak, but her chest tightened so that she could barely breathe. She hadn't had a panic attack in months now, but she felt the beginnings of one and bit down on her lip.

"Yes." The word was barely a whisper.

The deputy had been leaning over her, but at her reply he frowned and squatted down beside her. "What happened?"

Cheyenne took a deep breath and stared into his eyes. "I think someone wants to kill me."

Sandra Robbins is an award-winning, multipublished author of Christian fiction who lives with her husband in Tennessee. Without the support of her wonderful husband, four children and five grandchildren, it would be impossible for her to write. It is her prayer that God will use her words to plant seeds of hope in the lives of her readers so they may come to know the peace she draws from her life.

Books by Sandra Robbins

Love Inspired Suspense

Smoky Mountain Secrets

In a Killer's Sights
Stalking Season

Bounty Hunters

Fugitive Trackdown
Fugitive at Large
Yuletide Fugitive Threat

The Cold Case Files

Dangerous Waters
Yuletide Jeopardy
Trail of Secrets

Visit the Author Profile page at Harlequin.com for more titles.

STALKING SEASON

SANDRA ROBBINS

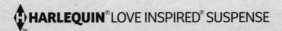

HARLEQUIN® LOVE INSPIRED® SUSPENSE

Recycling programs
for this product may
not exist in your area.

 LOVE INSPIRED BOOKS

ISBN-13: 978-0-373-67794-8

Stalking Season

Let us draw near with a true heart in full assurance of faith,
having our hearts sprinkled from an evil conscience,
and our bodies washed with pure water.
—Hebrews 10:22

Dedicated to the 6.6 million people who,
according to The National Center for the Victims of Crime,
are stalked in one year in the United States.

ONE

Cheyenne Cassidy ambled down the aisle of the Smoky Mountain Christmas Store and hummed along with the sound of Bing Crosby crooning "White Christmas" over the store's intercom. With Christmas only a few weeks away, shoppers were out en masse today, and from what she'd been told by the locals the crowds would only get larger as more visitors came to the mountains in the next few weeks to see the decorations and take in all the Christmas festivities.

The smells of cinnamon, pine and peppermint drifted in the air from the different areas of the store. Cheyenne stopped and blinked back tears at the reminder of her childhood and how their house had always smelled during the holidays. Her mother loved Christmas and had always been determined that her family would make memories to last a lifetime. Unfortunately these days, she had many memories of happy times, but the people she loved were no longer present to share them with her.

The world as Cheyenne had known it had come to an abrupt halt six months ago with the deaths of her parents. Alone in the world and with her life in shreds, she'd done the only thing she could think to do—follow the rodeo circuit. Without her parents, though, it also had lost the allure it had once had. Now she was far away from the home she'd always known and starting a new life in a resort town in the Smoky Mountains. She'd wanted to settle somewhere, and the Smoky Mountains seemed the perfect place to do that.

She sighed and walked down the aisle of a row of tall showcases holding all kinds of stuffed animals and dolls in Christmas outfits. The shelves in the case were packed with toys, and the display reached higher than her head. She stopped to stare at a teddy bear with a red ribbon around its head, and she suddenly stilled as her cell phone chimed that she had an incoming text message. She stared at the unfamiliar number displayed on the screen and frowned as she realized it was a video text.

With a frown she tapped the screen, and the recording began to play. For a moment all she could do was stand there, her mouth hanging open and her body shaking. Her knees wobbled, and she reached out to grab a shelf to keep from falling. She blinked, in the hope that what she was seeing and hearing wasn't really there, but she knew that wasn't the case.

Her eyes grew wide as the camera zoomed in on a tabletop, where a small, wooden music box sat. The top was lifted, and the tinkling melody of "Jack and Jill," the nursery rhyme she and her father had sung together so many times, drifted out. The tune wasn't what caused her breath to hitch in her throat, though. It was the fact that she knew right away that this wasn't just any music box. It was the one her father had bought for her on her eighth birthday. The one that had disappeared from their house two years ago. The one she'd always known *he* took.

But it couldn't be him. He was dead. The police said so.

With shaking fingers she stopped the video, but immediately the sound of another incoming text message from the same unknown number chimed. Swallowing the fear that gripped her,

Cheyenne opened the text and stared at the words that seemed to wiggle on the screen. I've missed you. See you soon.

A scream rose in her throat, and she clamped her hand over her mouth to keep it from escaping. She didn't need all the clerks and customers rushing to her side and demanding to know what was the matter. Only a few people in this town knew her story, and she wanted to keep it that way.

She took a deep breath and removed her hand from her mouth. With her gaze still fixed on the words on the screen, she bit down on her lip. *Calm down*, she told herself. *This isn't from him*. It could be anybody who knew what had happened and was playing a sick joke.

Suddenly a feeling that she was being watched swept over her. She'd had this happen many times in the past when he was stalking her, but it hadn't happened since her parents' deaths. She shook her head in denial. No, he was dead. He had to be dead. She couldn't go through this anymore.

At that moment her phone chimed again, and she looked down at it. Swallowing the fear that rose in her throat, she opened the text.

I like that scarf you're wearing. The blue color brings out the highlights in your hair.

Her hand began to shake, and panic gripped her heart. With a swift twist of her head she looked around to see if she could detect someone watching her. There was no one, but suddenly she heard footsteps on the other side of the tall display case beside her. The smart thing to do would be to go to the end of the aisle and face whoever was there, but she'd learned two years ago that when it came to him, she wasn't smart. She was scared, and she had to protect herself.

She looked up and down the aisle to see if anyone else was nearby, but she seemed to be alone in this part of the store. She turned and hurried in the direction she'd come when entering the store. Before she could reach the exit, her phone rang with an incoming call. Against her better judgment, she connected the call.

"H-hello."

"It's good to hear your voice, Sunshine."

Her skin prickled, and she stood frozen in place, unable to move. The sickening feeling she'd experienced so often in the past spread through her, and she knew with certainty this wasn't someone just trying to scare her. It really was *him*. Only he knew that nickname. It was the one he'd given her. Sunshine, because he said she'd lit up his world. For her it had only brought darkness into her life.

"You're not dead." She meant it to be a question, but it came out as a statement.

"No. Disappointed?"

"Leave me alone," she whispered. "I don't want to do this again."

"You have no choice in the matter," the familiar voice whispered. "Just like I had no say when you decided to break up with me for someone else."

Her heart pounded, and she wanted to run, but her body wouldn't respond. "Why can't you understand that we were never together?" she pleaded.

A long sigh echoed in her ear. "Keep telling yourself that but you and I know the truth. I know you left quite a bit out of your story when you talked to the police."

A sob escaped her mouth. "Please, leave me alone."

"You led me on, Cheyenne, and broke my heart. That's what I told your parents right before I killed them."

Tears began to roll down her face. "Please…"

"They're dead because of what you did. You made me become a killer, but I've decided to forgive you. Because I love you, I'm going to give you one more chance to make it up to me for everything you've done to me. Don't disappoint me this time."

Her knees shook so hard that she thought she was going to collapse. "Don't you come near me again, or I'll go to the police."

He laughed, and the sound sent chills down her back. "A lot of good that did you the last time. I'm back, and I'll be watching you. Soon we will be together for always."

"Leave me alone!" she yelled into the phone and then disconnected the call.

She stood there for a moment before she looked around and noticed the two young women at the checkout counter staring at her with their eyes wide. "Is something the matter?" one of them asked.

Without answering, Cheyenne bolted toward the exit, shoved past a customer who was just entering the store and ran out the door. Once on the sidewalk she cast a nervous glance at her truck at the far end of the parking lot. Her only thought was that she had to get there.

Without looking in either direction she

dashed into the street and realized her mistake too late when the sounds of a honking horn and screeching brakes caused her to glance to her right. She barely had time to register the fact that she was in the path of an oncoming car before she felt the impact of the vehicle.

Her feet lifted off the street, and then she was hurtling through space. She landed in the other lane of traffic, facedown on the pavement. The next thing she knew she was staring at a man's shoes beside her face. She turned her head so that she could look up. A man with his hands on his knees hovered over her.

"Ma'am, are you all right?" She could hear concern in the man's voice, and his smooth Southern drawl had a comforting effect.

Unable to answer, she planted her palms on the pavement and succeeded in pushing up to a sitting position. "I—I think so," she murmured.

She looked down at her jeans and saw a hole in the knee. The skin underneath the fabric burned, as did the palms of her hands. "Sit still," the man's voice said again. "I've called for paramedics. They should be here any minute."

For the first time she looked into the face

of the man bending over her, and her heart skipped a beat at the blue eyes staring down at her. She let her gaze drift lower, and she sucked in her breath at the fact that he was wearing a police uniform.

She raised a shaky hand to her forehead and closed her eyes. "Oh, thank goodness," she said. "I ran into the path of a police car."

The man's eyebrows arched. "Thank goodness? Are you sure you're all right?"

"I think so," she said as she started to get up.

He laid a restraining hand on her arm. "Ma'am, you've just been hit by a police car. You may be all right, but I have to make out a report on this accident, and I have to know for sure. Please don't move until the paramedics get here. I'm sorry I didn't see you in time to stop, but you ran right out in front of my car. Can you tell me your name?"

She frowned and rubbed at her forehead, which was throbbing. She flinched when her fingers touched the spot, but the skin didn't feel broken. Probably a scrape from sliding on the pavement. She swallowed and looked back up at the officer. "I'm Cheyenne Cassidy."

"And do you know where you are?"

She nodded. "I'm sitting in the street in front of the Christmas store where I was shopping."

"Do you know what day it is?"

A smile pulled at her mouth, and she looked up at him. "I know you're trying to determine if I've been knocked senseless, Officer, but I assure you I know where I am and what has happened. Now may I ask who you are?"

"Deputy Luke Conrad, ma'am. Why were you in such a hurry?"

The question sent a wave of fear rushing through her as she recalled what had occurred before she ran onto the street, and she glanced back at the store. A crowd had gathered at the front door. They all seemed to be staring straight at her. She scanned the group but didn't see a familiar face. But how could she tell who he was? In the two years she'd endured the terror of a stalker, she'd never seen his face.

How could he be alive? And if he was, how did he find her now?

"Ma'am…" The deputy's voice interrupted her thoughts. "Did something happen that frightened you? Is that why you ran in front of my car?"

She tried to speak, but her chest tightened so that she could barely breathe. Her body began to shake as tears filled her eyes. She hadn't had a panic attack in months now, but she felt the beginnings of one and bit down on her lip.

"Yes." The word was barely a whisper.

The deputy had been leaning over her, but at her reply he frowned and squatted down beside her. "What happened?"

Cheyenne took a deep breath and stared into his eyes. "I think someone wants to kill me."

Luke Conrad tried to hide his surprise at the woman's words, but from the way she was staring at him, he wasn't sure he was successful. He glanced back at the crowd gathered in front of the store and scanned the faces there. Nothing seemed out of the ordinary, and he didn't recognize anyone.

He waved a hand in their direction and called out in a loud voice. "Okay, folks. You can go on about your business now. Those Christmas gifts aren't going to get bought if you keep standing around out here."

The low rumble of voices drifted across the parking lot as the crowd dispersed and turned their attention away from the woman sitting in the middle of the street. She glanced at the departing onlookers before she looked back up at him, her lips quivering in a shaky smile. "Thank you. I was beginning to feel a bit embarrassed sitting here."

"There's no need for that, ma'am. They were just interested in what was going on." He paused for a moment. "But suppose you tell me why someone is trying to kill you."

"I didn't say he was trying to kill me, I said I think he wants to kill me."

Luke frowned. "And what makes you think that?"

She started to respond, but the ambulance arrived at that moment. Two EMTs jumped out when the vehicle came to a stop, and he stepped back to give them better access to examine her. After about fifteen minutes, they both stood and helped her to her feet.

"You seem to be fine, Miss Cassidy," one of the paramedics said, then grinned. "Just watch where you're going from now on."

"I will. And thanks for checking me out, guys."

"It was our pleasure," the other said and glanced at Luke. "She seems to be fine, Luke. Just some abrasions that should heal on their own."

"Thanks, Joe. Good to see you."

"You, too," he said as he and his partner headed back to the ambulance.

Luke watched the ambulance depart before he turned back to her. His squad car still sat in the middle of the street, and he nodded toward it. "Now suppose we sit down in my car and you tell me about this person who wants to kill you."

She nodded and took a deep breath. "It's a long story, and at the moment I don't know where to start."

"Then maybe we need to go to the sheriff's office so you can take all the time you want. Do you mind doing that, ma'am?"

She closed her eyes for a moment and pursed her lips. "Would you please quit calling me *ma'am*? You're making me feel like I'm a little old lady that a Boy Scout is trying to help across the street."

His eyes grew wide for a moment, and then he threw back his head and laughed. When he'd quit shaking, he smiled at her. "I'll try, but old habits are hard to break. Here in the South we use those terms out of respect a lot." He studied her for a moment. "What part of the country are you visiting the Smokies from?"

"Actually, I'm not visiting. I just moved here."

"You did? What brought you to this area?"

"I—I came to perform at the Smoky Mountain Wild West Show."

His eyebrows arched. "You're a cowgirl?"

She looked down at the jeans, Western-styled shirt and boots she was wearing, and a grin pulled at her lips. "Well," she said, "dressed like this I doubt anybody would mistake me for a Southern belle."

His face warmed, and he swallowed. "I guess you're right, but I have to say you're pretty enough to be one." He bit down on his tongue and struggled to think of something to say that would ease his embarrassment. "I'm not saying that cowgirls aren't pretty. I'm just saying…" He paused, and her grin grew larger. After a moment he smiled, too. "I guess you know what I'm saying," he finally said.

"I do, and thank you for the compliment."

He looked down at the information he'd written when he first talked to her. "So your name is Cheyenne Cassidy, you've just moved to this area and you think someone wants to kill you. Are you okay with going to the station to give me your statement?"

She nodded. "I am. My truck is parked over there. Should I follow you?"

"No. You're still a bit shaken. Why don't you ride with me? I'll bring you back here when we're finished."

She hesitated a moment before she smiled. "Okay, Deputy Conrad. I can do that."

He opened the passenger-side door of his car and she climbed in. Then he walked around, got in behind the steering wheel and drove out of the parking lot into the heavy traffic that was clogging the main street in town today. He hadn't seen this many tourists since the summer, but he was glad they had come. The local economy could always use the boost from sales, and Christmas was one of the busiest times of the year for the shops and attractions in this area.

He came to a stop at a red light, and as the car idled, he found his thoughts returning to the young woman sitting silently beside him. He'd heard the expression "deer in the headlights" all his life and had experienced having to swerve around a big buck in the middle of a mountain road several times, but now he really knew what it meant.

When she had run in front of his car, she had looked frightened, more like terrified, and her big brown eyes had stood out in her pale face. She'd dashed off the sidewalk as if she was being pursued by somebody and straight into the path of his car. And now he knew why. She said someone wanted to kill her, and he needed to find out why she thought that. But first he needed to put her at ease and convince her she could trust him.

He cleared his throat. "So, you're new to the Wild West show. I was there last night, but I don't remember seeing you. Did you perform?"

She shook her head. "I was there, but I didn't perform. I just helped out behind the scenes. Tonight is my debut. I'm a trick rider."

Her words shocked him, and he glanced at her. "Wow!" he exclaimed. "When I was in college, my roommate's girlfriend was a trick rider. We used to go watch her perform a lot, so I know it's really dangerous."

"It can be if you're not careful and if you don't have a well-trained horse. I've had my horse, Patches, ever since he was a colt, and we know each other well." Then to his surprise she said, "Maybe you can come watch us perform sometime, Deputy Conrad."

He smiled. "I'll do that. Sometime."

She didn't say anything for a moment, and then she spoke in such a soft voice that he almost missed what she was saying. "Thank you, Deputy Conrad, for everything. I appreciate your help today."

"Luke," he said. "Call me Luke. And it was my pleasure, Cheyenne."

"I was so scared when I ran out of that store. If I hadn't literally run into you, I don't know what I would have done."

He started to ask what she meant, but she turned her head and stared out the window. The light turned green, and he moved forward in the line of traffic. Two blocks later he turned right and pulled into the parking lot of the sheriff's department.

When he'd pulled to a stop, she turned to stare at him. The way she bit down on her lip, and the way her eyes sparkled with unshed tears, made his heartbeat race. Something was terribly wrong. He didn't know what it was yet, but there was one thing he did know: Cheyenne Cassidy was scared, and he had to find out why her face had the same terrified look as when he'd first seen her through the windshield of his car.

"This is the sheriff's office," he said, "and I promise you we'll do everything we can to put you at ease."

She took a deep breath and nodded. "Then it will be the first time I'll feel that way in two years."

He started to ask her what she meant, but she was already climbing from the car. He opened his door, jumped out and caught up to her when she rounded the front of the vehicle. "I'm sure everything's going to be okay."

She looked up at him for a moment and then shook her head. "My parents did, too, and now they're dead."

Before he could respond, she walked past him and pulled open the door to the building. He didn't move for a moment and then strode after her. His mind whirled with all the things she'd said since they'd met. Something told him he was about to hear a story that was different from anything he'd experienced since becoming a deputy in this small mountain community.

TWO

Cheyenne stepped inside the building and stopped as Luke walked up beside her. A dispatcher at a desk in the entry looked up from her computer and smiled as they entered. The woman pushed a lock of gray hair out of her eyes as her gaze swept over Cheyenne and came to rest on Luke.

Her face lit up with a friendly smile. "Hi, Luke. You back for shift change?"

Cheyenne looked up at the deputy and frowned. "You didn't tell me you were about to go off duty. I don't want to delay you. I can give my statement to another officer, and you can go on home.

He shook his head. "It's no big deal. We stay past our shift all the time if we're trying to help someone in trouble." He looked back at the woman behind the desk. "If Sheriff Whitman comes in, tell him I'm in the interrogation room taking a statement from Miss Cassidy. If he wants to join us, he can."

The woman leaned forward with her arms folded on her desk as she smiled at Cheyenne. "Cassidy? Are you the trick rider who's staying with Dean and Gwen Harwell out at the Little Pigeon Ranch?"

The question stunned Cheyenne, and her eyes widened. She'd been in town less than a week, and this woman already knew about her. Coming to the small resort town of Pigeon Forge had seemed like a good way to lose herself in all the tourists who poured through here each year, but perhaps she'd been wrong.

Cheyenne swallowed before she spoke. "Yes. How did you know?"

The woman waved her hand in dismissal. "This is really a small town, and all the locals know each other."

Luke frowned and placed his hand on Cheyenne's elbow. "And Clara knows everybody's business." He pointed down the hall. "Our interrogation room is down here. Let's go in there so we can talk."

Cheyenne looked over her shoulder as Luke guided her away from the desk. Clara had stood up and was watching them walk away. Her arms were crossed, and a smug smile pulled at her mouth. Cheyenne turned her attention back to Luke as he stopped and opened the door. "Here we are. Would you like something to drink before we begin? I can get you a soda from the vending machine or a cup of coffee, but I have to warn you that by this time of afternoon the coffee is strong enough to make a spoon stand up in it."

Cheyenne smiled and shook her head. "No, thanks. I'm fine."

"Then go in and have a seat."

She stepped into the small room and surveyed the space. It looked very much like the interrogation rooms she saw on the TV detective show she watched. A table with four chairs sat near one corner of the room and a mirror that appeared to be built into the Sheetrock covered most of the wall opposite.

Luke nudged her to the table and pulled out her chair, but she couldn't take her eyes off the mirror. "I suppose that's a two-way mirror. Is there someone on the other side watching us?"

He shook his head. "No, but I can't promise you there won't be by the time we get through. If Sheriff Whitman comes in, he may go in there instead of disturbing us. I will tell you, however, that there is a camera in the corner, and it will be recording our conversation. Is that all right with you?"

She shrugged. "I suppose so. Once I make a statement, it will on record anyway. This isn't my first time to talk to a police officer."

Luke's eyebrows arched. "Really? And when was the first time?"

She sighed, closed her eyes and rubbed her hand across her forehead. "I suppose the best place to start is at the beginning—two years ago."

Luke opened a notepad and wrote something before he glanced back up at her. "Go on."

Cheyenne took a deep breath. "Well, we've already established the facts that I am Cheyenne Cassidy, I moved here a few weeks ago to become a trick rider with the Wild West show and, as Clara has let you know, I'm living at Little Pigeon Ranch."

A smile tugged at his mouth. "Clara is very good at her job, but she has a nose for news. She keeps up with everyone in town. Don't take offense."

"I won't. It just surprised me that she knew." She settled back in her chair. "I moved to Pigeon Forge from Wyoming. My family raised horses on a ranch there, and my father coached the rodeo team at a college nearby. Ever since I can remember, my parents competed in rodeos. My mother did barrel racing and my father was a bronc rider. I started doing trick riding when I was young and began performing on the circuit with them when I was still in elementary school. I've been doing it ever since, until recently, when I decided to give it up."

"Why did you quit?"

Cheyenne closed her eyes and let the memories she tried to keep at bay enter her mind. "About two years ago I started getting anonymous messages and flowers, always white roses, from a secret admirer. Everywhere I went I felt like I was being followed. Sometimes I would catch a glimpse of a man in the shadows, but he was smart enough not to let me ever see his face. At first his messages were filled with words of how much he loved me, but that all changed when I starting dating a cowboy on the rodeo circuit. Then they became threatening and filled with ultimatums."

"What kind of ultimatums?"

"He'd write things telling me I was his and if

I didn't want something to happen to my boyfriend, I'd better break up with him."

Luke quit writing and looked up at her. "So what did you do?"

Cheyenne's shoulders sagged. "I broke up with him. I was about to have a nervous breakdown, but that didn't stop him. He broke into our house several times when we were away. The last time he did, he completely destroyed my room. The only thing missing, however, was a music box my father had given me years before."

Luke glanced up at her and pursed his lips. "It sounds like he was following a pattern."

"What do you mean?" Cheyenne asked.

"There are stages that stalkers progress through when they become obsessed with someone. The early stages include things like uncomfortable contact, intimidation and then threatening messages. Things begin to get out of hand when the stalker starts to destroy personal property."

Cheyenne's eyes narrowed, and she nodded. "That's exactly how it progressed over a period of two years, but the police could never catch him. Then six months ago my mother and father left for a rodeo, but I didn't go. He'd sent me a note telling me that we were finally going to meet, and I was scared. I stayed with some friends. While my folks were at the rodeo, somebody broke into the trailer where they were sleeping and murdered both of them."

Luke's lips clamped together and his Adam's apple bobbed as he swallowed. "They were murdered?" he asked as if he couldn't believe what she'd just said.

"Yes."

"Did they find out who did it?"

Cheyenne shook her head. "That's still a subject for debate. The police suspected it was the man who'd been stalking me because the killer left a note saying that their deaths were my punishment because I'd been unfaithful to him and hadn't come to meet him. There were white roses scattered over my parents' bodies."

"So your stalker killed your parents."

"That's what the police thought. A few days after the murder, they found the body of Clint Shelton, a rodeo worker, in his truck. He'd left a note saying he couldn't live with himself any longer, that he'd killed my parents because I had rejected him."

"You don't sound like you're convinced this Shelton guy did it."

She shook her head. "It just never made sense to me. I barely knew Clint. He was one of the best hazers in the business, but we weren't friends. He was engaged to be married, so I couldn't understand why he would become fixated on me."

"But the police disagreed?"

"Yes. The detective who was in charge of the case was eager to close it, and he took the suicide note as proof that Clint was the killer. There was no DNA or any physical evidence that put him at the scene, though."

Luke sat back in his chair a moment and stared at her as he tapped the pen he held on the desk. "Wow, I can't believe all this. You've been through a terrible time."

Cheyenne nodded. "Yes, I have. I tried to stay on the rodeo circuit, but after a few months I knew it would never be the same without my parents. That's when Bill Johnson, who owns the Wild West show, contacted me. He was a friend of my father's. In fact, his son Trace was on the rodeo team my father coached, and he has always been a close friend of mine. They wanted to help me put all my bad memories behind, so they offered me a job. Trace got it arranged for me to live out at Dean and Gwen's ranch."

After a moment Luke leaned forward and tilted his head to one side. "So I suppose that brings us to today. What happened that made you run into traffic without looking at where you were going?"

A chill ran up Cheyenne's back as she recalled the incident inside the store. Then she began to speak, and the words poured out of her. She told him of the video of the stolen music box, and the cryptic text messages and phone call that told her he was going to give her one more chance to be with him.

"He accused me of being the reason my parents were dead, that I had turned him into a killer. But he said that he'd forgiven me and was going to give me one more chance to be with him." She blinked back tears. "The way he said it made me think that if I rejected him again I would pay for it. That sounds like a death threat to me."

Luke nodded. "It does to me, too. I think you should take this warning seriously."

She held up her hands in despair. "But what can I do? He's eluded everybody for the last two years. I don't want to move again to try and hide from him. I want this nightmare to be out of my life."

"I understand," Luke said, "and our department will do everything we can to make sure you're protected. I think you should think about postponing your debut at the Wild West show until we know more about what's going on."

Cheyenne shook her head. "I can't do that. Bill has advertised that Cheyenne Cassidy, three-time women's winner in the International Trick Riding Competition, will be making her debut appearance. He's almost sold out for tonight's performance, so I can't let him down."

"Still," Luke began, "I think—"

She pushed to her feet and clasped her hands in front of her. "I know you're trying to help, and I appreciate it. But I need to get through tonight and then decide what I'm going to do."

He stared at her for a moment as if he was going to argue. Then he let out a deep breath and pushed to his feet. "Then let me suggest that you stay close to someone you know. Don't be alone at any time, and as soon as the show is finished, go home."

"I can do that."

"Good. Then I'll come by Little Pigeon Ranch tomorrow and check on you."

Neither one of them said anything for a few minutes as they stared at each other. Then Cheyenne stuck out her hand and tried to smile. "Thank you, Deputy Conrad, for being so nice to me today. I appreciate your concern, and I promise I'll be very aware of my surroundings."

His fingers wrapped around hers and he smiled. "I thought you were going to call me Luke."

Her face grew warm and she tugged her hand loose. "Okay. Luke it is."

"I'll drop by the ranch tomorrow and see how things are going with you. In the meantime, don't hesitate to call if you need me." He pulled his card from his pocket and handed it to her. "My number's on there, and you can call me anytime."

"Thank you. I'll keep that in mind."

Luke cleared his throat and held out his hand toward the door. "Now if you're ready, I'll drive you back to your truck."

A slight frown pulled at her forehead. "Don't you need to clock out of your shift? I can wait until you get done."

"I'll come back and do that after I deliver you to your truck,"

"Very well. Let's go so you can get back. I'm afraid I've already delayed you long enough," she said as she headed toward the door.

"It goes with the job, Cheyenne." She gave a nod and turned toward the door, but his voice stopped her. "One more thing. Would you mind giving me your cell phone? I'll have our tech guys check it to see if they can trace where today's texts and calls came from."

"Sure," she said as she pulled it from her pocket and dropped it in his hand.

His fingers closed around it. "I'll get this back to you as soon as I can."

"I'm glad for you to have it if it will help any."

They didn't speak again as they walked back to his squad car. The traffic wasn't as bad as it had been earlier, and before she knew it they'd reached the parking lot where she'd left her truck. When the cruiser stopped, Luke swiveled in the seat, looped his arm over the steering wheel and smiled. "It's been a pleasure meeting you even if I did almost kill you. I hope we meet under happier circumstances."

Her heart gave a small lurch at the way his eyes sparkled as he looked at her. "I hope so, too," she said. She opened the door and stepped out of his car.

A few minutes later she was in her truck and driving down the main thoroughfare of town. She looked in the rearview mirror and smiled at the sight of Luke trailing along behind her in his car. When she came to the turnoff to the road that would take her to the ranch, she glanced back again. He flipped the headlights on and then off, as if he was signaling goodbye, and then he drove away toward the police station.

For the first time in years she felt a small prick of something that might be called pleasure. It had been so long since she'd had anything to be happy about that she almost didn't recognize it. Then she smiled. If Luke Conrad was any indication of the kind of people who lived in this area, then she was going to enjoy being here.

As suddenly as the thought struck her, she shook her head and gritted her teeth. There was never going to be happiness in her life until the monster who'd stalked her and killed her parents was behind bars. Maybe then she'd be able to live a normal life like other people. But until then she had to be on her guard every minute. She couldn't let thoughts of handsome deputies or anything else blind her to the fact that she was never going to be safe until her mysterious stalker was caught.

Luke's thoughts centered on Cheyenne Cassidy all the way back to the sheriff's office. He couldn't get the young woman with the flashing brown eyes and silky auburn hair out of his mind. With her jeans and boots she'd certainly looked like a cowgirl, but there was a fragile quality about her that made his breath catch in his throat.

He groaned and raked his hand through his hair. What was the matter with him? He would not let himself repeat the mistake he'd made when he'd first become a deputy. He'd been warned not to become personally involved with the people in his cases, but he hadn't listened.

He'd let his heart rule his head when he'd taken a special interest in Jasmine after she'd been robbed at gunpoint at the convenience store where she worked.

She had seemed fragile, too, and she'd turned out to be about as delicate as an 18-wheeler. She'd leaned heavily on him for support in the weeks following the robbery, and he'd fallen head over heels for her. He'd thought she cared for him, too, until the day the owner of the convenience store called to say that Jasmine was missing along with a hefty sum of money from the cash register.

She and her male companion were arrested a few weeks later in South Carolina. They'd been stopped for a traffic violation and a bench warrant for Jasmine's arrest showed up when they searched her name. It didn't take long for her to confess that the man with her was the one who'd robbed the convenience store, and she'd been in on the robbery all along.

After that, Luke had decided he was going to be careful. His job was to offer professional help—and nothing more. There would be no other Jasmines for him. He liked his life too well the way it was now to put himself through something like that again.

There was no doubt, however, that Cheyenne needed help, but right now he wasn't sure how to proceed. He pulled into the parking lot and sat there a moment recalling all the things Cheyenne had told him, then got out and walked inside. Clara still sat at her desk and looked up as he came in the door. When he walked inside, she looked up from her computer and smiled. "Hi, Luke. Are you ready to clock out?"

"Not yet. I have some reports to finish."

"Okay," she said as she leaned forward in her chair and glanced from side to side as if to see if anyone was listening. Then she spoke in a soft voice. "I noticed when I came in this morning that there had been a call about a domestic disturbance over at Bruce and Linda Carter's house last night. Ben took the call, but he didn't say much about it. Did you happen to hear anything today?"

Luke tried to keep from grinning. Clara had a reputation in town as the local gossip, and she was always on the lookout for more information. Ben Whitman, the sheriff, had warned her several times about questioning the officers about the calls they answered, but it did no good. Clara felt it was her duty to keep the good folks in town aware of what was going on around them.

"Sorry, Clara, I haven't heard anything about that. I'm sure if it was anything serious Sheriff Whitman would have told you."

She settled back in her chair and pursed her lips. "I suppose so, but I never have trusted that Bruce. He drinks a lot. I don't know why Linda puts up with it. Now if that was my husband—"

"Excuse me, Clara," he interrupted, "but I have some work to do before I leave. I'll talk to you later."

He took a step to leave but stopped when she spoke again. "Did you get Miss Cassidy back to her truck okay?"

He turned slowly to face her and nodded. "She's on her way home right now."

"That's good. That poor child looked like she was scared to death when she walked in with you. I hope you were able to calm her down. After all she's been through it would be a shame if she didn't get to perform tonight."

Luke cocked an eyebrow. "Now why doesn't it surprise me that you know all about Cheyenne?"

Clara waved her hand in dismissal. "Oh, I know all about her stalker, and about her parents being killed, and how she's come here to forget the past and work at the Wild West show."

Luke shook his head in amazement. He'd often said that the government should hire Clara as a spy. She could infiltrate a country and have all their secrets in no time at all. "How did you find all that out?"

Clara crossed her arms as a smug smile curved her lips. "Shorty, the cook out at Little Pigeon Ranch, told me."

Luke chuckled and shook his head. "Shorty probably didn't stand a chance against you once you decided he needed to spill the beans about the new resident at the ranch. But tell me, Clara, did you happen to get her birth date and social security number while you were at it?"

Her mouth dropped open for a moment, and then she scowled at him. "Are you making fun of me, Luke Conrad?"

He held his hands up in a defensive move. "Not at all. I'm just in awe of all your interrogating skills. I think Ben needs to promote you to detective."

She glared at him. "You *are* making fun of me."

Luke laughed and shook his head. "I'm just teasing. You know I love you like a sister. I just wish that Cheyenne had come to town under different circumstances."

"Yeah," Clara said. "I told Shorty the same thing. He said she'd been real private ever since she got here, acted like she didn't want to make friends."

"Maybe Dean and Gwen can help change that."

Clara looked at him, and a sly grin spread across her face. "Are you thinking maybe you could help change that, too?"

Luke felt his face flush, and he shook his head. "I didn't say that. The job of this department is to make her feel safe."

Clara arched her eyebrows and rolled her eyes. "If you say so."

He started to respond, but he just frowned and huffed out a breath as he turned and strode down the hallway toward his office. When he walked in, he headed straight to his desk and slumped down in the chair behind it. He sat there in thought for a moment before he straightened and prepared to fill out the reports he had to file. He needed to hurry or he'd be late getting home tonight, and that wouldn't do if he was going to get to the Wild West show. He wasn't going there to see Cheyenne ride. He would probably need to return her cell phone if the techs had finished with it.

At least that's what he told himself as he began to fill out his reports.

THREE

Cheyenne drove the truck up the long driveway that led to the main house on Little Pigeon Ranch. She pulled to a stop in front, turned off the ignition and sat there a few moments letting her gaze drift over the rambling structure that now served as a lodge for guests who wanted to experience the adventure of being on a dude ranch.

She smiled as her eyes moved over the house and the cabins scattered across the fields nearby. After a few weeks this place was already beginning to feel like home, especially since Patches was with her and they had a place to train. It was hard enough leaving her family ranch behind and all the memories of her parents associated with the place. She didn't think she could have endured it if she'd had to leave her horse, too.

When her father's friend and his son had offered her the opportunity to ride in the Wild West show, she thought that would be the answer to getting on with her life and leaving the past behind. Now she wasn't so sure. The texts and the phone call this afternoon had signaled that the terror she'd lived through wasn't over after all.

Even though she'd had trouble believing her parents' killer was really dead, she'd been comforted by the fact that he hadn't contacted her in all these months. Now he was back, and this time it seemed worse than ever.

His threatening words had played over and over in her mind all the way home. No matter how much she tried to convince herself that it might have been a copycat intent on scaring her, she couldn't bring herself to believe that. For one thing, he had her music box, and for another the guttural voice had sounded the same.

If he was alive, as she now believed him to be, he had not just murdered her parents, but probably Clint Shelton, too, in order to evade suspicion. If that was true, then Clint had been an unknowing victim in a vicious game that some crazed person had started two years before.

All the top steer wrestlers had wanted Clint as their hazer. His death had stunned the rodeo regulars, who found it hard to believe such evil could be buried inside a man who was so respected and well-liked. That's why it had never made sense to her that he would have been her stalker and killed her parents.

She sighed and shook her head, then climbed from the truck and started toward the house. She stopped when she heard a shrill voice ring out across the yard.

"Cheyenne! Wait for me!"

Cheyenne turned to stare in the direction the voice had come from and spotted Maggie Harwell, Dean and Gwen's six-year-old daughter, with a tan-and-white collie running alongside her from the direction of the barn. She barely had time to brace herself before the child plowed into her and wrapped her arms around Cheyenne's waist. She looked down into Maggie's smiling face and hugged her.

"That's quite a welcome, Maggie," Cheyenne said. "If I'd known you'd be this excited to see me, I would have come back sooner." The collie jumped up on Cheyenne, and she reached out and patted the dog's head. "I'm glad to see you, too, Bingo."

Maggie's brown eyes sparkled as she looked up at Cheyenne. "Mama and Daddy said they would take me to see you ride tonight. I'm going to yell and clap louder than anybody else there."

Cheyenne laughed and released Maggie. "I'll listen for you."

"I'm sure you'll be able to hear her above everybody else."

Cheyenne looked up to see Dean Harwell coming toward them, a smile on his face. She hadn't been at the Little Pigeon Ranch long, but she had already begun to feel like everybody here was family. Dean and Gwen had accepted her right off and made her feel like this was her home. She and Maggie had bonded right away, and Cheyenne had grown accustomed to seeing the little girl sitting on the ground outside the corral during her practice sessions with Patches.

She and Maggie turned to face Dean as he came to a stop beside them. "Thank you for coming tonight," she said. "It means a lot to me that you'll be there. You're the only people

I've really met since I moved here, and you're beginning to feel like family."

"We feel the same. It's good to have you here," he said as he reached down and lifted his daughter so that she sat on his shoulders with her legs dangling over his chest.

Maggie squealed in delight and took hold of her father's head as the three of them walked up the steps to the house. Once inside he deposited Maggie back on her feet, bent over and kissed her on the cheek. "Why don't you go see what Shorty's cooking up for dinner? Cheyenne will need to eat early so she and Patches can get into town and be ready for the show's grand opening."

"Okay," Maggie said and started to run toward the kitchen. At the door she stopped and looked back at Cheyenne. "Are you going to do the hippodrome stand tonight?" she asked.

Cheyenne nodded. "Yes, that's what I'm going to open with."

Maggie directed a somber stare at her father. "That's the one where Cheyenne stands up on the saddle while Patches runs around the ring."

Dean arched his eyebrows, but Cheyenne could see the corners of his mouth trying not to smile. "Really?"

Maggie nodded and turned back to Cheyenne. "What about the side shoulder stand?"

"I plan to do that one, too." She smiled at Maggie. "You've been watching me practice so much you know all my tricks."

A small frown flitted across her face as if she'd just had a troubling thought. "I don't like the suicide drag. Don't do it tonight."

Cheyenne glanced at Dean and then at Maggie. She walked over to the child and put her arm around her. "I know that trick scares you, but it's the highlight of my performance. You don't have to worry. Patches is well trained, and that's the secret to doing this trick. If it scares you, though, just cover your eyes, and it'll be over in minutes. Okay?"

Maggie smiled a wobbly smile and nodded before she turned and ran toward the kitchen with Bingo right behind her.

Dean didn't take his eyes off her as he watched her go, then he turned back to Cheyenne. "She's grown very attached to you since you've been here. Thanks for letting her hang around while you train."

Cheyenne waved her hand in dismissal. "No problem. I enjoy having her there. I find myself checking my watch to see when she's going to get off the school bus so I can see her." She paused for a moment. "I also enjoy being here with you and Gwen and Shorty and Emmett and all the people who work here. I haven't felt so comfortable in a long time."

"We're glad to have you. There's something about living in the Smoky Mountains that makes a person think they've come home to the place where they were meant to be."

Cheyenne nodded. "I know. I'm beginning to feel that way."

"Well, you and Patches are welcome to stay here as long as you want." Dean took a deep breath. "So how did the shopping trip go?"

Cheyenne hesitated for a moment and swallowed hard before she answered. "I-it was fine."

Dean directed a sharp look at her and cocked an eyebrow. "Did something happen?"

She shook her head. "Nothing for you to worry about."

She started to walk away but Dean reached out and touched her arm. "Cheyenne, I used to be a police officer. I know when there's something bothering a person. Did you have some kind of problem?"

For a moment she debated what to say. Dean

and Gwen knew her story, but she didn't want to put them or their child in danger by keeping silent. "I kinda got hit by a car," she said.

"Did you have a fender bender? I didn't see any damage to your truck when you drove up."

"No. I walked out in front of a car without looking, and it hit me. Fortunately, I wasn't hurt."

Concern lined his face, and he studied her as if searching for injuries. "Are you sure you're all right? Gwen is in the kitchen. She can take you to our doctor to get you checked out."

Cheyenne shook her head. "That's not necessary. Luke called 911, and the paramedics checked me out. They said I was fine."

"Luke?"

"Yes, Luke Conrad. He's the one who hit me." She bit down on her lip as her face grew warm. "He was in his patrol car."

He stared at her for a moment. "Luke Conrad is a friend of mine. I hope you won't blame him."

"Oh, I don't. It was all my fault. I should have been watching where I was going."

Dean studied her for a moment. "I have the feeling that there's more to the story. What aren't you telling me?"

Before she realized what she was doing, she began to tell Dean the story of what had happened in the store. When she finished, she flinched at the grim expression on his face. "I'd say this is serious, Cheyenne, and we can't take it lightly. We need to find this person whether he's your stalker or somebody trying to scare you."

"I know that, Dean. But I don't know where to start. Luke made me promise to call if I needed him."

"It goes without saying that you can do the same with us. I don't want anything to happen to you. You've suffered enough from this guy. It's time he was stopped." He paused a moment. "Maybe you don't need to ride until we know for sure what's going on."

"I can't drop out right now. My appearance has been advertised, and I don't want Bill to have to deal with any disgruntled customers who come to see me. Don't you worry. I'll stay close to the other performers and keep an eye out for anything out of place."

Dean frowned and shook his head. "I don't know, Cheyenne. I think you should postpone your appearance."

"I'm sorry, but I can't do that." She took a

deep breath. "Now I'm going upstairs to get my fancy costume with all the glitter on it, and then I'm going to load Patches in my trailer. Then if Shorty has anything ready, I'll grab something to eat. I need to leave and get to the arena early so that I can get Patches used to the place before the show starts."

Before Dean could protest, Gwen walked into the room from the direction of the kitchen. A worried look lined her face as she wiped her hands on a dish towel as she approached. "Cheyenne, I didn't know you were home." She walked over, grasped Cheyenne's arms and stared into her face. "Are you all right? I just heard about your accident."

Cheyenne's eyes grew wide with disbelief. "You did? How did you know about it?"

"Clara, the dispatcher at the sheriff's office, called and told me. She said Luke Conrad brought you in to make a statement about it."

Cheyenne frowned and looked from Dean to Gwen. "I don't understand why she'd call to check on me. I only met her this afternoon."

Dean chuckled. "Oh, I expect it was more than a friendly check on how you were doing. She was trying to find out how you were so she could broadcast it to the rest of the locals."

"Broadcast it? You mean she's like on the radio or TV?"

Gwen laughed. "No, but she's quicker than any text message you've ever seen. She knows everything that's going on and makes sure everybody else does, too."

"Oh, I see."

Gwen crossed her arms and smiled. "In fact she seemed to think that Luke Conrad was quite smitten with you."

"Well, I don't know where she got that idea," Cheyenne said in a huffing voice. "I gave him my statement, he drove me back to my truck and I came home. That's all there was to it."

Dean held up his hands in front of him and nodded. "Okay, if that's the way you want it. But folks around her are friendly, and you'll find that you'll like a lot of them, Clara included. And Luke is a great guy. You'll really like him when you get to know him."

"Thanks. But I don't plan on getting to know him. I'm content just to be here with all the people at Little Pigeon."

"Whatever you say," Gwen said as she looped her arm through her husband's and smiled up at him. "Why don't you come out to the kitchen, Dean, and help Shorty and me get dinner ready? We have quite a few guests eating with us tonight."

He leaned over and kissed his wife on the cheek. "Anything for you, darling."

She laughed, and they turned to walk toward the kitchen. Gwen suddenly stopped and looked back over her shoulder. "Oh, I forgot, Cheyenne. You have a letter on the hall table."

Her body stiffened, and the muscles in her back and shoulders tensed. Who could know where to send her a letter? "Mail? For me?"

Gwen nodded. "Yes. I left it there for you."

Cheyenne waited until Gwen and Dean were out of sight before she walked to the table in the hallway where a small, sky blue envelope with her name and the address of the ranch on it lay. Her fingers shook as she picked up the letter and stared at it for a moment. Then, she took a deep breath, ran her fingernail under the flap and opened the envelope. It contained a single piece of paper of the same color.

The letter was folded in half, and she hesitated a moment before she unfolded it. For a few seconds all she could do was stare at the image of a white rose at the top of the page. She began to shake as her eyes traveled down to the words written beneath it.

"No, no, no, no," she whispered over and over as she staggered backward until she felt the wall behind her. She took several deep breaths and looked down at the letter still clutched in her hand.

Hello, darling. I'll see you soon.

No matter how much she might want to believe he was dead, he wasn't. He was right here in the mountains, where she'd escaped to in hopes of finding peace, and he wasn't going to leave her alone until he got what he wanted. This time he wasn't going to be satisfied with stealing items from her room or following her wherever she went. She had no doubt this time he meant to kill her.

Luke Conrad glanced at his watch as he hurried toward the building that housed the indoor arena for Bill Johnson's Smoky Mountain Wild West Show. It had taken him longer to finish his work at the sheriff's office than he'd thought, and he had rushed to get here on time. Even with traffic as heavy as it was in town tonight, he still had about fifteen minutes before the show started.

He was happy to see the parking lot was filled with cars. Judging from all the shoppers he'd seen today while he was on duty, and the cars and trucks that clogged up the main drag of town, it looked like this Christmas season was going to be a successful one for the local residents.

He hurried as he approached the entrance to the arena and stepped through the door into a wide lobby that housed the ticket windows and some concession stands. The smell of popcorn filled the air and he smiled as he saw a group of children, each armed with a paper cone of pink cotton candy in one hand a box of popcorn in the other. They pushed and shoved each other as they were herded toward the arena by several adults who already looked weary.

Luke stepped up to the first ticket window, smiled at Josie Hatcher—the wife of Brent Hatcher, one of his oldest friends—and handed her the money for his ticket. "Hi, Josie. One, please."

Josie grinned at him and slid one ticket and a program across the counter. "I keep thinking that one of these days you're going to surprise me and buy two tickets. There are plenty of girls in town who'd love to come to the show with you. Why don't you break down and ask one out? You might find you really like it."

He smiled and shook his head. "Since Brent took you out of commission I haven't been able to find anybody," he teased.

She laughed and shook her head. "You'd better watch out. You're not getting any younger, and one of these days when you least expect it some girl is going to have you lassoed and hog-tied before you know it."

He arched his eyebrows and tried to look horrified. "I don't think so. Not if I can help it."

Josie's eyes darkened and she tilted her head to one side. "Luke, you know Brent and I are some of your oldest friends. All I'm saying is that not every woman is like Jasmine. You just have to keep looking."

Luke's face grew warm, and he scowled. "I'm not interested in looking." He exhaled and picked up his ticket. "Is Brent riding tonight?"

Josie nodded and sighed as if she knew it was time to change the subject. "Yes, he's leading the opening parade, and he's driving in the buckboard shuffle tonight. We have some wranglers who work behind the scenes, so he'll spend most of his time keeping everybody on time backstage."

"Well, if you see him, tell him to keep an eye out for Cheyenne Cassidy tonight."

A worried expression flashed on Josie's face. "Why? Is something wrong with her?"

"No. It's her opening night, and I covered a small accident she had this afternoon."

"Oh, I see," Josie said as she gave him a quizzical look. "So this is work-related, a deputy sheriff following up on a case."

His face burned, and he wondered if it had turned red. "Something like that," he mumbled as he turned away from the ticket counter and caught sight of Dean and Gwen Harwell, and their daughter, at the concession stand. As he walked toward them, the girl working there handed Maggie a big cone of cotton candy.

He eased up behind Maggie and leaned over. "Are you going to share that with me?"

She turned to face him and gave a squeal of pleasure before she threw her arms around his neck. "I didn't know you were going to be here."

He gave her a swift hug and smiled. "Well, I am, and if it's okay with you, I'd like to sit with you and your folks."

"Oh, yes." She glanced up at Dean. "It's okay if Luke sits with us, isn't it?"

Dean laughed and reached out to shake Luke's hand. "Of course he can."

Luke smiled at Maggie and then glanced at Gwen. "Hi, Gwen. It's good to see you again."

A smile pulled at her lips, and she and Dean exchanged a glance before she spoke. "I thought you might be here tonight."

His forehead wrinkled. "Oh? What made you think that?"

"Well," she said, "Cheyenne Cassidy is making her debut tonight, and I knew the two of you met this afternoon."

His face grew warm, and he swallowed. "Yeah, she was involved in a little accident. I took the report."

"From what I hear," Dean said, "there was a little more to it than you taking a report."

Now his face felt hot. "Uh, I guess you could say that. She kinda stepped out in front of my car, and I kinda hit her."

Dean laughed. "Then why don't we go get our seats so we can all see Cheyenne make her debut."

Luke was thankful the conversation had steered to safer ground, and he nodded and followed the Harwell family into the arena. They found seats very quickly several rows up on the bleachers that ran along side the paneled wall of the arena. They'd barely gotten settled when the lights dimmed, and a man's voice came over the intercom. As he began to speak, the audience quieted, and all eyes were trained on the far end of the arena, where he stood on a small stage. On either side of the stage were large doors that Luke knew would serve as the entrances and exits for the horses.

"Ladies and gentlemen, welcome to Bill Johnson's Smoky Mountain Wild West Christmas Show in our 38,000-square-foot arena right here in the heart of the Smokies. Tonight we celebrate the holidays with this special show that's designed to thrill you, no matter how old you are. Get ready for a night of horsemanship, spectacle, special effects, music and danger as you witness our cowboys and cowgirls thrill you with their daring rides at top speeds that will leave you shaking your heads in disbelief."

With that the music swelled, the doors on either side of the stage swung open and a line of horses entered the arena in single file. The sequins on the riders' costumes sparkled from the spotlights, and each rider held a pole that was stuck in a holder near the stirrup. A white flag covered in white sequins fluttered from each pole as the horses made their way into the arena and circled it at a slow gait. Beside him Maggie pulled on his sleeve and pointed toward the riders.

"There's Cheyenne!" she cried out as she gestured wildly in her direction.

Luke nodded. "I see her."

At that moment the music softened, and on cue Luke's friend Brent Hatcher turned his horse toward the exit, and the others followed. He watched Cheyenne ride her horse out of the arena and then turned his attention to the first act.

Since Luke had seen the show the night before, he settled back in his seat and spent the next thirty minutes more interested in Maggie's reaction to the various acts taking place on the arena floor. From time to time when Maggie let out whoop of delight, he saw Dean and Gwen exchange smiles. Something in the way they stared at each other made him wistful.

He'd thought he'd that once with Jasmine, but he'd been wrong. In his mind he knew all women weren't like her, but his heart cautioned him to be careful. He couldn't be hurt again if he played it safe, and that was what he intended to do. That meant he wouldn't be testing the waters with any woman. Not now, and maybe not ever.

At that moment Maggie grabbed his arm and cried out in a shrill voice, "It's time for Cheyenne!"

He jerked his attention back to the announcer, who had stepped to the small stage again. "And now, ladies and gentlemen," he declared in a booming voice, "get ready for the thrill of a lifetime as the Smoky Mountain Wild West Show presents the debut of our newest trick rider. From Jackson Hole, Wyoming, riding her horse Patches, put your hands together and give a big Smoky Mountain welcome to three-time women's international trick-riding award winner Cheyenne Cassidy!"

The crowd roared its approval as one of the doors at the end of the arena swung open. Luke gasped as Cheyenne's horse galloped at top speed into the arena with her standing on the saddle. Her costume glittered as if she was wearing diamonds, and next to him he heard Maggie yell.

"Go! Cheyenne! Go!"

Luke smiled at the excited look on Maggie's face and he cupped his hands around his mouth and gave a loud cheer as Patches raced around the arena.

Maggie leaned close to him and yelled so he could hear her above the roar of the crowd. "That's a hippodrome stand. It's one of my favorite tricks."

"I like it, too," he said as his gaze followed Cheyenne, who now had shifted her position. With one hand on Patches's mane and the other on the saddle horn, she shifted her position until she stood with one leg on the saddle, her arms spread out to the side and her other leg extended backward.

"That's a crane stand," Maggie yelled over the noise.

Luke nodded, but he couldn't take his eyes off Cheyenne as she stood perched like a crane on the saddle while the horse galloped at top speed around the arena. And then just as quickly she transitioned back into the saddle. In the next instant she vaulted from the saddle to the ground, pushed up and landed back in the saddle. The crowd gasped and then broke into thunderous applause.

Suddenly he saw Maggie turn to Gwen and bury her face against her mother. He frowned and glanced at Gwen. "What's wrong?" he asked.

"Maggie's seen Cheyenne practice her performance so many times she knows that she's getting ready to do the suicide drag, and she doesn't like to watch that," Gwen answered.

"And now," he heard the announcer bellow, "get ready for the death-defying ride of the night as Cheyenne and Patches attempt the dangerous Cossack drag, or known to some as the suicide drag!"

Luke had seen stunt riders perform this trick before, and he watched as Cheyenne stuck her right foot through the drag strap attached to her saddle and lean to the left until her right knee was in line with the saddle horn. Then in one swift motion she twisted her body so that she hung down the left side of the horse, her left leg suspended at a ninety-degree angle from Patches, and her hands dragging along the ground.

He turned to Maggie to assure her that there was nothing to be afraid of when a sudden gasp from the crowd jerked his attention back to the arena. His eyes grew wide and his mouth dropped open as Cheyenne's body slipped farther down the side of the horse, shifting her weight even lower. He'd been around horses all his life and knew the sudden change was enough to pull Patches off balance and bring him down to the ground on top of Cheyenne, who was trapped with her foot inside that drag strap.

With a lurch Patches stumbled and struggled to keep his balance. But it was no use. His legs buckled, and he fell to the arena floor, taking Cheyenne with him. Luke jumped up from his seat and pushed between the people on the bleachers in front of him. When he reached the arena fence, he grabbed the top panel and pulled himself over. Then he ran toward the spot where Cheyenne and Patches both lay on the arena floor.

He saw no movement, and as he sprinted toward her, all he could do was pray that she was still alive.

FOUR

Cheyenne could hear someone calling her name, but the sound seemed to be coming from far away. She slowly opened her eyes and flinched as the bright lights from overhead almost blinded her. When a figure above her blocked the light, she stared up into the most beautiful blue eyes she'd ever seen. Somehow they seemed familiar.

She frowned and searched her memory and then realization dawned. "Luke," she whispered as she tried to push into a sitting position. "What happened?"

Luke put his hands on her shoulders and eased her back down to the ground. "Don't move," he cautioned. "You've had a fall."

She rubbed her hand over her forehead and closed her eyes. "A fall?"

"Yes," another voice beside her said. She turned her head to see Trace Johnson on her other side. "Lie still until the paramedics get here. We need to make sure that you're not injured."

"Trace, really. I think I can get…"

Before she could move, he gripped her arm. "Please, Cheyenne. It's our policy that every rider is thoroughly examined when something happens during one of our shows. You need to do as I ask."

With a sigh she sank back down to the ground. "Okay, if you insist."

"I do."

"And he's right," Luke said. Again, just as it had done earlier today, his Southern drawl soothed her.

She looked up at him and smiled. "I know. It's just embarrassing being gawked at again."

Luke grinned. "And this time you have a much larger crowd."

She was about to respond when from somewhere close by, Patches whinnied. She jerked her head toward the sound. "Patches!" she cried. "What's wrong with Patches?"

"He fell, too," Trace said. "But don't worry. Our vet is with him now. And here come the

EMTs to take care of you. I'll go check on your horse and let you know how he is."

"I'm going to get up and let the paramedics take charge, Cheyenne, but I'll be right here," Luke said as he released her hand.

For a moment she felt as if she was alone. Then someone kneeled down beside her, and another familiar face came into view. "Well, well, Miss Cassidy. We've got to quit meeting like this." Joe the EMT, who'd answered the call earlier today, smiled down at her. "You certainly have made my day at work more interesting," he said as he began to check for broken bones. "If it wasn't for you, I might have spent the whole shift watching soap operas and reality shows on TV."

Cheyenne couldn't help but smile. "I'm sorry to be such a bother, but I feel fine." She heard Patches whinny again, and she jerked her head around toward the sound. "What's happening to my horse?"

Joe turned and glanced in the direction of the sound. "Don't worry. The wranglers are getting him up now. Looks like he's heading back to the stalls. Trace is going with them, too. I'm sure he'll let you know how your horse is as soon as he knows anything. Now just relax and let me finish checking you out."

For the next few minutes as Joe performed his examination, she felt as if they were doing a replay of her earlier accident. When he'd finished, he sat back on his heels and smiled. "Everything looks good so far. But we'll know for sure after we get you to the hospital."

"The hospital?" she cried. "I can't go to the hospital. I need to see about Patches."

She tried to push up again, but Joe put his hand on her shoulder to restrain her. "I can't let you do that, Miss Cassidy. I don't think you have any severe injuries, but I have to let a doctor exam you."

Cheyenne shook her head. "No. I have to see about my horse."

"We'll take care of Patches," a deep voice beside her rumbled.

She looked up at Bill Johnson, the show's owner and Trace's father, staring down at her. "Really, Mr. Johnson, I feel fine," she said.

His gaze raked her face. "That may be, but I need to make sure. I insist that all our performers are checked out after an accident. Besides, if your father was here, he'd tell you the same thing."

The mention of her father brought tears to her eyes. He and Mr. Johnson had become good friends when Trace was on her father's college rodeo team.

She bit down on her lip and nodded. "You're right."

"I insist, too," a familiar voice said as someone clasped her hand. She looked up into Gwen's smiling face. Dean stood behind her with a sobbing Maggie in his arms, and suddenly she didn't feel alone. Dean and Gwen were here, and her new friend Luke Conrad had been the first one to reach her. Then there was Joe, who'd taken care of her twice today, and Trace Johnson, who'd been her friend for years, was looking after Patches.

"I'm very lucky to have people who care," she said.

The next thing she knew the other EMT arrived with a gurney, and he and Joe lifted her carefully onto it. When she was settled on it, she turned her head and stared at Maggie, who was still sobbing with her head buried on her father's shoulder.

"Maggie," she said. "Please don't cry. I'm okay."

Maggie lifted her head and stared at Cheyenne. A big tear slid out of the corner of her eye and down her cheek. "I told you not to do that trick. It scared me. I thought you were going to die."

She reached toward Maggie, and Dean held his daughter down so Cheyenne could grasp her hand. "I'm okay. Now you quit crying and go on home. I'll see you as soon as I get there."

Maggie scrunched her eyebrows and she gave a little hiccup. "Do you promise?"

"I promise. I'll see you and Bingo as soon as I get there."

Gwen, who stood next to the gurney, nodded. "I think Maggie does need to go home. I'll take her, and Dean can drive your truck. He can pick you up at the hospital and bring you home."

"I'll be glad to do that," Luke said. "If Dean will drive Maggie's truck home, I can bring Cheyenne when the doctor releases her."

"You'll go to the hospital with me?" Cheyenne asked.

Luke grinned. "I've reported one accident you've been in today. I may as well do this one, too."

Cheyenne laughed as Joe finished tucking a blanket around her. As they started across the arena to a waiting ambulance, the announcer's voice boomed out on the intercom. "Ladies and gentlemen, Cheyenne appears to have no injuries, but she's being taken to the hospital as a precaution. Let's send her off with a big Smoky Mountain round of applause with our best wishes."

A roar went up from the crowd, and Cheyenne waved from the gurney as she was lifted into the back of the ambulance. Luke climbed inside and bent over her while Joe was getting her settled. He smiled again, and for the first time she noticed a little dimple in his right cheek. "I'll come to the hospital as soon as I know how Patches is," he said. "In the meantime Joe will take good care of you."

A chuckle rumbled from Joe's throat. "Of course I will. Miss Cassidy is fast becoming one of my favorite patients."

Cheyenne looked from Luke to Joe and fought back the tears that threatened to slip from her eyes. "You've both been great to me today, and I appreciate it. I dreaded moving here, but I'm beginning to be glad I did."

Luke smiled, and his eyes softened. "We're

glad you did, too." Then he cleared his throat and backed away. "I'll see you at the hospital."

"Would you mind doing me a favor?" she asked.

"Sure. What do you need?"

"My coat with my wallet in the pocket is hanging in Bill's office. Would you get it and bring it to the hospital? I'll need my insurance cards."

"No problem. I'll take care of it."

"Thanks, Luke. See you there," Cheyenne said as Joe closed the back door.

As the ambulance began to move, Cheyenne lay there thinking about what had happened in the arena tonight. She couldn't understand it. In all the years she and Patches had been performing that trick, they'd never had an accident. Until tonight.

She raised her hand to her forehead and rubbed it. It all seemed like a blur. Everything had been going well, then suddenly she and Patches were falling.

Had she done something wrong that caused them to fall? Was she the reason her horse was hurt? He was her best friend, the only thing she had left from her old life, and she couldn't live with herself if she had made a mistake that caused him to be injured. Her chest tightened at the thought, and she bit down on her lip.

Not another one. She closed her eyes, but the words flashed in her mind like a blinking sign.

She tried to shut the words from her mind, but as usual they refused to go away. She'd tried over and over to ignore them, but it was no use. They were a constant reminder of the secret that had tormented her for the past year. The guilt she already carried was difficult to live with, but she didn't think she could bear to add Patches to the list of her victims, too.

Luke stood in the parking lot of the Wild West show and watched the ambulance head down the street on its way to the hospital. When he couldn't see the taillights any longer, he turned and walked back to the area behind the arena where the horses and equipment for the show were kept.

In true showmanship, the performance was proceeding as planned, and he walked past a line of horses and riders who were prepared to ride through the arena's entrance as soon as they were introduced. He'd been in this behind-the-scenes barn area many times, and he knew where the vet would be examining Patches.

He strode down the alleyway between stalls until he arrived at the exam room at the back of the barn. Dean stood outside looking in, and Luke stopped next to him. Inside the room Dr. Sherman, the local veterinarian and the one who took care of all the show animals for the Johnsons, was bent over studying Patches's legs. Bill and Trace Johnson stood behind him, watching. "What does Doc say about Cheyenne's horse?" Luke asked.

"Nothing yet," Dean said. "He's still checking him out. He should be through in a few minutes."

They stood there in silence as they watched the veterinarian working with the horse, and then Luke turned to Dean. "I haven't figured out yet how that accident could have happened. Everything seemed to be going so well, and then all of a sudden it fell to pieces."

Dean nodded. "I know. I've been thinking about it, too. I've watched Cheyenne train with Patches ever since she's been here, and I know how careful she is. She never takes a reckless chance, and she makes sure her equipment is in good shape before using it."

Luke glanced around and spotted the tack that Cheyenne had used draped over a saddle stand in the corner of the exam room. He turned to Dean. "Have you looked at her equipment to see if it malfunctioned?"

Dean shook his head. "No, I thought you might want to do that. One of the cowboys who led Patches in here took the saddle off and left it over there."

"Well, let's take a look at it," Luke said.

Trace and Bill both turned to stare as Luke and Dean walked into the room and stopped at the saddle stand. "What are you doing?" Bill asked.

"Just want to examine Cheyenne's equipment," Luke answered.

Bill nodded. "I was going to do that myself, but go ahead. See if you can find out what might have caused the horse to fall."

Luke picked up the bridle and examined the headstall, bit, chin strap and reins.

"These all look good," he said after a few minutes.

"What about the brow band and the nose strap?" Dean asked.

"They're okay, too," Luke answered. "Maybe it was the breast collar. If something happened that made it slip, it could have caused the saddle to shift." He picked it up and searched every inch of it, but it appeared in good shape. "Nope, not the breast collar."

Dean exhaled a long breath. "Then maybe it was the cinch. If the girth under Patches's belly had torn, that would have caused the saddle to slip." He picked up the band that holds the saddle on the horse's back and examined it, then shook his head. "It looks good, too."

Luke took a step back and let his gaze drift over the tack. "There has to be something."

Dean pushed the cowboy hat he wore back on his head, propped his hands on his hips and exhaled a deep breath. "But what?"

Luke shook his head. "I don't know, but… Wait a minute. There's one thing we haven't examined yet. The drag strap. Maybe something happened with it. All the tricks had gone off without a hitch until she started the suicide drag."

"Good idea." Dean pointed to the white leather strap that was still buckled to the right side of the saddle. "Take it off so you can look at it up close."

Luke bent over the saddle stand and was about to unbuckle the strap when he stopped and stared at it. When he didn't say anything, Dean stepped closer and peered over his shoulder. "What is it?"

Luke pointed to the strap's buckle. "Look at the holes that the buckle's prong fits through."

Dean looked at it a moment. "What do you see?"

"The prong is in the first hole of the strap, but the leather between it and the third hole is torn. It looks like maybe the prong had originally been placed in the third hole, but it slipped up two holes, loosening the strap."

"I haven't had much experience with trick riding. What are you saying?"

Luke pursed his lips and stared at the drag strap for a moment before he spoke. "I'm saying the strap was no longer adjusted to her height, which means her foot would have slid up the horse's side because of the shortened distance. So as her right leg moved farther up Patches's body, she couldn't bring herself back up into the saddle, and she dropped closer to the ground. Once that happened her knee wasn't lined up with the saddle horn anymore, and Patches was thrown off balance. That's what brought him down."

Dean leaned closer and stared at the strap.

"Luke, that doesn't look like a tear. If it had torn, the line left would show evidence of it having ripped, but this is smooth. Like it's been cut with a knife. Do you think someone did this on purpose?"

Luke nodded. "That's exactly what I think. But who would want to do something like that?"

"Do what?" Trace Johnson asked from behind.

"Sabotage Cheyenne's equipment so she would have an accident," Luke said.

Trace's mouth dropped open, and he looked from Luke to Dean as if he couldn't believe what he'd heard. "You can't be serious. Cheyenne hasn't been here long, but everybody really likes her. And we don't allow anybody back in the stall area except our employees."

Luke nodded. "I know. That's why this doesn't make any sense, but the fact is that this strap was tampered with sometime before the performance." A sudden thought popped into his head, and he turned toward Dean. "Did Cheyenne tell you about our encounter in the parking lot at the Smoky Mountain Christmas Store this afternoon?"

"She did."

"And about the statement she gave me?"

"Yes. We already knew her story, and she was still very upset when she got home. I tried to discourage her from riding tonight, but it was no use. She was determined to do it."

"I know," Luke said. "Even though the paramedics didn't think she was hurt, she was knocked quite a distance when I hit her with my car."

Trace's eyes grew even larger. "You hit her with your car today? She didn't say a thing to me or to Dad about it."

Luke rubbed his chin and stared at the drag strap. "It happened in front of that Christmas store at the mall. It was an accident, but what happened tonight wasn't. Somebody cut that drag strap, and she was almost killed. When a trick rider's foot is in a drag strap, they're stuck there. I don't know how she managed to get her foot out of it, but she did, and it saved her life. If she hadn't been thrown clear of the horse, he would have come down on top of her."

Trace looked at him as if he couldn't believe what he was hearing. "You're saying that someone deliberately did that to hurt her?"

Luke glanced back down at the strap. "More like somebody wanted to kill her."

Trace raked his hand through his hair and frowned. "I can't believe one of our employees would do something like this. What do we need to do, Luke?"

Luke took a deep breath. "Well, I'll need to question the wranglers working back here and see if anyone remembers seeing somebody hanging around Cheyenne's horse. Since they're all working, that can wait until later. Right now I think we need to find out how Patches is, then I'll go to the hospital to see about Cheyenne."

Trace let out a deep breath. "Well, we'd appreciate it if you'd keep this as quiet as possible. We can't afford to let word get out that our show's performers aren't safe. It could cause us a lot of problems."

Luke was about to respond, when a loud whinny sounded. All three of them turned around to see the veterinarian running his hands down Patches's left leg. "There, there, boy," the vet said. "I'm not trying to hurt you."

After a few moments he stood and stepped back from the horse, but continued to stare at the leg. Dean walked over to him. "What's the problem, Doc?"

Dr. Sherman took a deep breath and shook his head. "I can't be sure until I do an ultrasound, but I think we have a suspensory ligament injury," he said.

Luke and Trace joined the group standing around the horse, and Luke let his gaze move up Patches's left leg. "I've heard of that happening," he said. "The suspensory ligament is the one that extends from just below the knee down to the ankle and helps support the horse's weight, isn't it?"

The doctor nodded. "That's right. I think the tear in the ligament may be in one of its branches. The leg is warm, is sensitive to touch, and there's some swelling beginning to appear. Like I said, I'll know for sure once I do an ultrasound at my clinic."

"Cheyenne is going to be upset about this," Dean said. "What's the treatment, and what's the prognosis for an injury like this?"

"Well, of course I'll prescribe some anti-inflammatory drugs, but he'll also need cold therapy several times a day. That will include icing or hosing down, and then there will be stall rest. As the ligament starts to heal, he'll need some hand-walking every day for therapy. Then depending on how severe the injury, we may be able to ease him back into being ridden after several months."

"Several months?" Trace exclaimed. "You mean Cheyenne won't be able to work for a while?"

"Not unless she has another horse." The vet glanced at Dean. "Why don't we load him in Cheyenne's trailer and take him to my clinic? He can stay there tonight, and if all goes well, you can take him back to your ranch tomorrow."

Trace nodded. "Okay, Doc."

Luke and Dean stood in silence as the veterinarian walked back to Patches and began to wrap the injured leg with a bandage. After a minute Luke looked at Dean. "I'll go to the hospital and check on Cheyenne if you'll see that Patches gets settled for the night."

"Okay. I'll drive Cheyenne's truck home. Are you sure you don't mind bringing her? I can go by the hospital and get her if you have something else to do."

Luke shook his head. "No, I want to make sure she's all right and fill her in on Patches."

Bill Johnson shook his head as he stared at

the horse. "I've had this show for years, and we've had a few accidents along the way. But never anything like this where foul play was suspected."

Trace laid his hand on his dad's shoulder. "Don't get upset. Luke will get to the bottom of this." He glanced at Luke. "I'm sure you'll file a report about this. What do you intend to say?"

Luke took a deep breath. "At this point I'm calling what happened tonight a suspicious accident, and I'm going to question Cheyenne to see if she remembers anything out of the ordinary happening in the backstage area before the show started."

Having said that, he turned and walked out of the barn area to the parking lot, where he'd left his truck. He could hear the excited cries and applause of the audience as the show continued. He'd come tonight just to see the young woman he'd met earlier today perform. Now he was on his way to the hospital to take a statement from her once again.

He had no idea how she would react when she found out that her horse had sustained an injury that would put him out of commission for several months. But that wasn't the worst news he had. It looked like she'd been right. Her stalker had returned, and he had delivered a life-threatening blow tonight.

With few clues to follow at this point, Luke had no idea where to start looking for him. But he did know one thing. He had to find Cheyenne's stalker before she ended up dead.

FIVE

Cheyenne shivered and pulled the covers up to her neck as she stared up at the ceiling from the bed where she lay. In the hallway outside the cubicle where she'd been deposited when Joe and his partner wheeled her through the emergency room door, she could hear the swishing of the nurses' shoes on the tiled hallway as they moved from one room to another. Christmas music, no doubt to put patients at ease, played softly over a sound system and drifted through the partially open door to her room.

However, it was going to take more than some holiday tunes to make her relax. All she could think about was feeling herself slip down Patches's side and knowing that they were going to fall. In those terrifying moments she had believed she would die with her beloved horse crushing her to death. She still couldn't figure out how she'd been able to free herself.

Finding out the answers was going to have to wait until she got out of here, and she needed to quit thinking about it for now. After being pricked, probed and delivered back from the X-ray department, she had nothing to do but be patient and await the final word from the doctor. She was eager to get back to Patches, make sure that he was all right and get them both home.

She heard heavier footsteps in the hallway and looked toward the door expecting to see the doctor. Instead she heard a soft tapping and a voice she immediately recognized. "Cheyenne, it's Luke. May I come in?"

"Yes, come in."

The door swung all the way open, and Luke stepped inside. Her gaze swept over his lanky figure as he walked toward her, and she smiled. Tonight he didn't have on his uniform but wore jeans and a Western-style shirt that was open at the neck. He held a Stetson in his hand and he smiled as he approached her bed.

"How are you feeling?"

"I'm fine," she answered. She motioned to a chair beside the bed as she pushed the button to raise the headrest. "Have a seat and keep me company until the doctor comes back."

He did so, placing his hat on the floor next to the chair, and leaned forward. He didn't say anything as she rearranged the pillows at her back and sat up straighter. When she looked back at him, he was studying her with an intense expression on his face. "Are you really all right?" he asked.

She laughed and finger-combed her hair. "I probably look a mess, but I'm okay. I just wish the doctor would come back and dismiss me. I'm ready to go get Patches and get home."

"That's one of the things I came to talk to you about."

The solemn look on his face frightened her, and her breath hitched in her throat. "Is something wrong with my horse?"

"I'm afraid it is."

She listened as he told her what the vet had said about the injury and the kind of care that the horse would need to have over the next few months. By the time he'd finished, tears were forming in her eyes. "This is all my fault. I must have done something to cause him to fall."

Luke's hand snaked out and covered hers.

"No. It wasn't anything you did. In fact it wasn't an accident at all."

The way he said it shocked her, and she felt her eyes grow wide. "What do you mean?"

"It wasn't your fault. Someone cut the drag strap, causing it to slip two notches."

It took a moment for his words to sink in, then her heartbeat accelerated. "Two notches? That means it wasn't adjusted for my height. When I slipped, I wasn't balanced, and I pulled Patches down."

Luke nodded. "Yes. If you hadn't kicked free of that strap somehow, you'd probably be dead by now."

She began to shake as her toes started to tingle with an icy feeling that slowly crept up her legs until it spread throughout her body. As the tremor increased, she felt the pressure from Luke's hand grow tighter.

"He's back. He's really back," she said with a sob. "I wanted to deny it, but I can't anymore. The police didn't find my parents' killer because he's still out there. And now he's determined that I'm going to be next."

"Cheyenne," Luke said, "our department will do everything we can to find him. Until we do, you have to be careful. You won't be able to perform because Patches is going to be out of commission for a few months, so you need to make sure that you stay close to someone at all times."

Tears rolled down her face, and she covered Luke's hand that still held hers with her free one. "If I could just make some sense out of it, maybe it would be different. But I don't know anything I've ever done to anybody that would make them do something like this."

He shook his head. "It's the same for all victims of a stalker. It's impossible to know what makes one person pick out another one to target. When they do, though, they make life miserable for their victim."

Cheyenne frowned and chewed on her bottom lip for a moment before she gazed back at Luke. "This afternoon at your office when I told you about my room being trashed, you mentioned something about how stalkers escalate through different stages. How would you categorize his actions now?"

Luke looked down at the floor as if he couldn't look her directly in the eye and shook his head. "Cheyenne, there's no need..."

She squeezed his hand tighter. "Tell me, Luke. I want to know."

He heaved a deep sigh and nodded. "The most dangerous stage is the last one. Once inanimate objects have been destroyed, the stalker only sees he has one option left. That's when he escalates to violence against a person. He's already killed your parents, but that didn't satisfy him. Now he thinks he's not going to be free until you are gone, too."

The longer Luke talked, the more frightened she became. "What am I going to do?" she whispered.

"The thing you can't do is panic. You have to keep control of yourself if we're going to catch this guy. Our sheriff has been in a meeting today over at Asheville, but he'll be back tomorrow. I've taken the drag strap, and I'll send it off to the state lab to see if there are any fingerprints on it, but I don't expect to hear from them anytime soon. They stay so backed up that it may be weeks. I'll talk to Sheriff Whitman when he gets home and see how he wants to proceed with this case. For now, though, let's just sit tight until the doctor dismisses you."

The words were barely out of his mouth when a knock on the door sounded, and the doctor walked into the room. Cheyenne had seen him earlier, and he had introduced himself as Dr. Wilson. He smiled as he stopped beside her bed. "Hello, Luke. I didn't know you were here."

Luke nodded. "I came to check on Cheyenne and to drive her home when you dismiss her."

The doctor held a medical chart in one hand, and he looked down at it before he responded. "Well, I don't think that's going to be tonight."

Cheyenne sat up straight in the bed. "What? I thought I'd go home when all the tests were done. Is something wrong?"

Dr. Wilson peered over the glasses that were perched on the end of his nose and smiled. "I don't think there's anything to get upset about, but you've had a hard fall. There's evidence of a concussion, and I would like to keep you in the hospital for observation overnight. If you appear to be doing well in the morning, you can go home. But there will be no trick riding or other strenuous activities for a while. Rest and medication are what you need."

"How long will my activities be curtailed?"

Dr. Wilson shrugged. "We'll just have to wait and see how you progress. It's in your best interests to follow my instructions."

Cheyenne started to object, but Luke spoke

up first. "You need to listen to Dr. Wilson, Cheyenne. I've known him for years, and he's very cautious with his patients. That's why everybody around here trusts him. You need to do that, too."

She settled back on her pillow and gave a sigh. "I know. I'm not trying to be difficult. It's just that this night has been very upsetting."

Dr. Wilson reached out and patted her hand. "I understand. Now just be patient, and the orderlies will be here in a few minutes to move you to a regular room. I'll see you in the morning."

"Wait a minute," Luke said before the doctor could leave the room. "There's evidence that Cheyenne's accident was a deliberate attempt by someone to sabotage her ride tonight. I want to make sure she's safe in the hospital. Do I need to have a deputy come sit outside her door, or can you get hospital security to take care of that?"

"I can do that. I'll contact our head of security, and he can assign one of his men to her floor for the night."

"Thanks, Doc. That makes me feel better."

Luke turned back to Cheyenne. "I'll stay with you until you're in a room and the security guy is outside. You'd better call Gwen and Dean and tell them you won't be coming home tonight."

The words were barely out of his mouth before he appeared to remember that he'd kept Cheyenne's phone earlier. His face flushed, and he reached in his pocket. He pulled it out and held it up. "Oops, sorry about that. I brought this with me tonight so I could return it to you."

She stared at the phone a moment, remembering how scared she'd been earlier today when she received the texts and the phone call. "Could your tech people tell where today's messages came from?"

He shook his head. "I'm sorry. They were sent from a burner phone, and they're impossible to trace."

She nodded, took the phone from his hand and tried to steady her shaking fingers as she scrolled to find the number, but it was no use. She had only begun to feel safe again, and now her stalker was back to get his revenge for what she had done. If she could only go back and undo the past.

Then suddenly a thought hit her, and she inhaled a quick breath. It wasn't the past she needed to worry about. It was the future and whether or not she would live to see it.

Luke waited until the nurses had gotten Cheyenne settled before he entered the room. She was on her cell phone talking to Gwen, and he tried to be quiet as he laid her wallet on the nightstand beside her bed. Then he walked to the closet and hung her coat inside. He'd just finished when he heard her end her conversation. He turned and walked back to the bed.

"What did Gwen say?"

"Nothing much. She was glad I was staying overnight and that Dean was at the barn. He and Emmett, his foreman, are trying to get Patches settled." Suddenly tears pooled in her eyes, and he couldn't help but notice how pale she looked lying there with her long hair spread out on her pillow.

He sat down in the chair beside her bed, reached over and squeezed the hand that lay on top of the covers. "Don't worry. The vet said Patches will be fine. It's just going to take some time."

A skeptical look crossed her face. "I've been

around horses all my life, and I know his injury could prove to be very serious."

Luke smiled. "Only time will tell. For now, though, you need to think about yourself. Are you hungry or maybe want a soft drink? I can get you something from the vending machine. It's in a room just around the corner at the end of the hall."

She shook her head, pulled the covers up and glanced at her watch. "It's late, and you've had a long day. Go on home. I'll be okay."

He shook his head. "I'll wait until the security officer gets here."

"Really, Luke," she insisted, "I'm fine. Go on and get to bed."

"Tomorrow's my day off, so don't worry."

She started to say something else, but before she could someone knocked at the door and it swung open. Bill and Trace Johnson, along with three of the wranglers from the Wild West show, surged into the room. They circled her bed and stood there staring at her. "What are you doing here?" Cheyenne asked as she looked at the faces gawking at her.

"We wanted to see how you're doing," Trace answered.

Her gaze darted from one to the other, and

Luke wondered if she remembered the names of the three cowboys with Bill and Trace. After all, tonight was her first time with the full cast. "Thank you for coming, but I'm all right. Just a little shaken up."

Luke stood up from his chair and shook hands with Bill and Trace. Then he stuck out his hand and moved to each of the cowboys. "Pete," he said. His handshake earned him a slight nod from Pete.

He turned to the next one. "Good to see you, Slim." He heard a grunt, and he almost smiled. Slim was known as having an ornery disposition, but Luke knew he had a strong protective streak when it came to the employees at the show where he'd worked for years.

When he got to the third one and shook his hand, the man flinched. Luke looked down at their clasped hands. "What's the matter, Virgil? You hurt your hand?"

Virgil's gaze dropped to his hand, and he tried to pull free. "It's nothing. I was trying to cut open a two-string hay bale, and my knife slipped. Nicked myself."

Luke studied the cut for a moment and then released Virgil's hand. "Better get that seen about. You don't want it to get infected."

Virgil nodded and stuck his hand in his pocket. "I'll put something on it when I get home."

"And home is where we all need to be, especially Trace. He's got a two a.m. flight out of Knoxville, and he needs to get on the road to the airport," Bill Johnson said. "They told us down in the ER you were being kept overnight, and we just wanted to see how you're doing or if you need anything."

"I'm fine," Cheyenne answered. "I'll talk to you tomorrow and let you know what the doctor said." She looked at Trace. "You're going somewhere?"

He nodded. "I'm going to Denver to look at some stock for sale that we may buy for the show. I booked a flight in the wee hours so I could work the show tonight. I have my bag in the truck, so I'm heading out as soon as we leave the hospital. I'll check on you while I'm gone."

She glanced at the clock on the wall. "I think you need to get on the road now so you won't miss your flight."

He grinned down at her. "Some things never change. You're still bossing me around." He bent over the bed and pressed his lips against

Cheyenne's forehead, before he pulled back and looked into her eyes. "You call me if you need anything, little sister."

She smiled up at Trace. "I will."

With that, the five men turned and shuffled from the room. When they'd closed the door behind them, Luke turned back to Cheyenne. "Little sister? What's that all about?"

Cheyenne wiggled back down under the covers. "I've known Trace for a long time. I think I told you he was on the rodeo team my father coached. At the time I was in high school, and I was kind of the mascot for the team. We became close friends and have remained that way through the years. Trace always teased me that I was like a bossy little sister that he'd always wanted, and the nickname stuck."

"I see." He didn't mean for the words to sound gruff, but he knew they did. There was no reason he should have a momentary jolt of jealousy at Trace Johnson's easy banter with Cheyenne. After all, they'd known each other for years, and he'd only met her today. Their time together ever since had been anything but easy. It had all centered around her fear of a killer who was stalking her.

"You're tired, and you've played nursemaid to me long enough today," she said, interrupting his thoughts. "Go on home and get some rest."

"Like I said, I don't want to leave until I know the security guard is on the floor. Let me check in the hallway and see if he's arrived."

Luke opened the door and looked out into the hallway. A man in a hospital security uniform leaned on the side of the nurses' desk as he stared down at a pretty RN sitting there. The nurse was laughing as if the man had just said something funny.

"Excuse me," Luke said. When neither one of them noticed him, he raised his voice. "Excuse me."

The guard turned around, and his eyebrows arched as he studied Luke. "Yes. Can I help you with something."

Luke pointed back to Cheyenne's room. "I'm Deputy Luke Conrad, and there's a patient in there who I want guarded all night. Are you the one who's supposed to do it?"

The man straightened and walked over to where Luke stood. "Yeah, I'm on all night. So I'll be right outside her door."

Luke tried not to frown as his gaze traveled

over the young man. He'd heard that the hospital hired college students to work at night, and he suspected he was one of them. At the moment he seemed more interested in the attention of the pretty nurse at the desk than he did in protecting a woman who'd survived an attempted murder tonight.

"You're going to sit outside her door?" Luke asked.

"Yeah. Housekeeping is going to send a chair up in a few minutes. I was just hanging here until it arrives. So you don't have to worry. You can go on home. Your victim is safe with me."

Luke hesitated a moment. He wasn't sure about leaving Cheyenne in the care of someone who gave the appearance of not taking his job too seriously. If he'd been trained better, he would have come in the room and assured Cheyenne that she had nothing to worry about instead of standing in the hallway flirting with a nurse. However, it would only strain relations between his department and the hospital administration if it looked like he was telling the man how to do his job.

He exhaled a deep breath and nodded toward Cheyenne's room. "Miss Cassidy has had quite a scare tonight. I just want to make sure that she's safe." He handed the young man his card. "If you have any problems, give me a call."

The guard took the card, studied it for a moment and then, with it grasped between two fingers, he lifted his hand to his forehead in salute. "Gotcha, Captain."

"Deputy Conrad will do," he said. "Now I'm going back in to tell Miss Cassidy good-night, and I'll see you when I leave."

"I'll be right here," the guard said with a smile.

Luke walked back into the room and stopped beside Cheyenne's bed. "The guard is outside, so I'm going on home. If you need anything, call the nurse or let him know. I'll come back in the morning to check on you and take you home."

"You don't have to do that. I'll get Dean or Gwen to come get me."

Luke shook his head. "They're busy in the mornings with their ranch guests. Since I'm off, I don't mind coming."

She seemed to debate whether or not she wanted him to come, but after a moment she nodded. "Okay. I'll see you then."

He nodded and walked back toward the

door. When his hand touched the knob to open it, he glanced back over his shoulder at her. She had sat up in bed and was staring at him, a slight smile on her face. In that moment it struck him that she had no family left. She was alone in the world.

At the thought a need to protect her poured through him, and he smiled. "Sweet dreams, Cheyenne. Don't worry about anything."

She just nodded as she continued to stare at him, and he turned back to the door. When he stepped into the hall, the guard was sitting in a chair outside her room. He looked up from a magazine he was leafing through and grinned. "Good night, Deputy Conrad."

Luke bit down on his lip, gave a curt nod and headed to the elevator. When the doors opened, he stepped inside. Just as he was about to push the button that would send him to the lower floor, he glanced back to where the guard had been sitting a minute ago. The chair was empty, and he could see him once again leaning on the nurses' desk talking to someone.

As the doors closed, he gave a deep sigh and shook his head. He'd told Cheyenne not to worry about anything, but he couldn't convince himself to do the same. He didn't feel comfortable at all leaving her here.

SIX

As soon as Luke walked out the door, Cheyenne closed her eyes and laid her head back on her pillow. A tear trickled out of her eye and ran down her cheek. She'd cried earlier but she didn't know how she'd been able to hold it together today without breaking down, but she had.

The discovery that her stalker was alive and back in her life had been enough to bring back all the horrible memories of the last few years, but tonight it had gotten even worse. He had tried to kill her.

She'd lived with the knowledge that he would do that sooner or later, but after Clint Shelton's body had been found with a suicide note she'd dared to believe her ordeal was over. It hadn't turned out to be that simple.

She bit down on her lip to keep from crying

out loud. She didn't want to alert the nurses that she was upset and have one of them to come scurrying in here. There'd been too many people fussing over her today. She didn't think she could bear one more, and she knew she didn't deserve another.

The thoughts running through her head had her keyed up, and she couldn't lie still. With a groan she threw back the covers and climbed out of bed. Without the warm blanket she'd been lying underneath, the room felt cold. The cotton hospital gown they'd put on her in the emergency room didn't offer much protection from the temperature in the room. She crossed her arms over her chest and wished for the warm, fleece robe that was hanging in her closet back at the ranch. If she didn't get to go home tomorrow, maybe Gwen would bring it and some of her personal items to the hospital.

Suddenly she remembered that Luke had brought her coat, and it was hanging in the closet. She grabbed it off the hanger and put it on—it was a long suede Western duster her parents had given her the Christmas before their deaths. For a moment she stood still, rubbing her hand over the soft material and the fringe that hung from the sleeves. She always felt close to her mother and father when she put on this coat, and tonight was no exception.

Without warning an excruciating pain seized her chest, and she doubled over. This had happened before, and she knew right away it wasn't caused by her accident. It was the festering guilt she carried inside that wanted to push its way to the top, and it was always a fight not to let it succeed.

Tonight she wasn't going to win that battle, and she gave in to the memories that began to flow through her mind. It seemed like only yesterday, but she knew it had been three years since she'd first met Jesse, or at least that's what he'd told her his name was.

She hadn't known what a nightmare her life would turn into when she first logged on to that online chat room, or she would have turned off her computer right away. It had been a lonely time in her life. So she'd taken the advice of a girl she'd met at the Calgary Stampede and joined a chat-room website.

That's when she met the man who called himself Jesse. It didn't take long for him to single her out from the group. He was looking for companionship, too, and right away they

became friends. They shared the same interests and moral beliefs, and they had a great
time joking and talking. Before she knew it,
she began to think of him as her best friend,
one she could tell anything to, and he seemed
to feel the same way.

They'd discussed meeting, but it never
seemed to work out. Their schedules con-
flicted, or he had to go out of the country on
a business trip, or one of his family members
needed him to help them with something. He
always had an excuse, and after a while she'd
grown tired of that. She didn't want a relationship in cyberspace. She wanted one with
a live person, and it didn't seem like that was
going to happen.

So after a year Cheyenne was ready to move
on. She'd met a young man who worked for the
local veterinarian, and they had begun dating.
Things were suddenly brighter in her life, and
she knew she had to end her online relationship with Jesse.

When she told him, he didn't react the way
she expected. His emails became filled with
anger, and his rants about how she'd been unfaithful to him scared her. As the weeks went

by, they grew more threatening, and she became even more frightened.

When his emails became threatening, she realized she was dealing with a psychopath. She had immediately quit answering his messages, but that hadn't deterred him, however.

She knew she'd been foolish to tell him where she lived when the white roses began to arrive. Then the threats had escalated to a physical presence. Everywhere she went, the feeling that he was always watching kept her on tenterhooks. After her room was ransacked, she'd known she was really in trouble. Then had come the phone call with the demand for her to meet him at the next rodeo, but she'd stayed home. Because of that, her parents had died, and it was all her fault.

The worst part of this whole sordid mess was her parents' murder. If only she'd told someone how it had all started, the police might have been able to catch him and they would still be alive. Instead she'd chosen to remain silent because she was embarrassed by how naive she'd been in her online relationship with Jesse.

That decision had led to her parents being killed, and she didn't think she would ever be able to forgive herself. It was a secret she would take to her grave.

Her chest tightened at the thought that even after all that had happened today, she still hadn't told Luke the whole truth. What would he think of her when he found out?

Cheyenne wiped away the tears that were rolling down her cheeks and buttoned the duster over her gown. She needed to get out of this room for a few minutes. Maybe a walk in the hall would calm her down. She remembered Luke saying there was a vending machine at the end of the hall. She grabbed some money from her wallet, which he'd left on the nightstand, opened the door and stepped outside.

A man dressed in a security guard's uniform stood at the nurses' station across from her room with his back to her. He was engaged in conversation with the nurse sitting at the desk, and they were so engrossed in what they were saying that neither one of them noticed her.

She didn't feel like answering any questions as to why she was out of bed, so she didn't speak and just turned in the direction Luke had said the vending room was located. At the end of the hall, she turned right, and there it was. She could see the lights of the soft-drink machine, but the room was dark otherwise. Something the staff probably did, she thought, because patients wouldn't normally be out of their rooms at this time of night.

As she stepped in, she noticed a door to the side. In the dim light from the machine she could barely make out the sign on it that identified it as a restroom. She stopped in front of the soft-drink dispenser and stared at the choices available. When she'd made a decision, she pushed her money through the coin slot and punched the button for her drink.

It rolled out and gave a thunk as it came to a stop. She bent over to pick it up but hesitated when the squeak of the bathroom door opening caught her attention. She straightened and started to turn around, but before she could, a hand clamped over her mouth. The breath was almost squeezed from her body as a strong arm circled her chest, pinning her arms to her sides.

Her body slammed back against the hard frame of a man, and her heart dropped to the pit of her stomach. She wanted to scream, but the hand over her mouth muffled her cries. She felt a warm breath fan the side of her face, and a voice whispered in her ear.

"Hello, Sunshine. It's Jesse."

* * *

Luke sat in his truck and stared at the entrance to the emergency room. For some reason he couldn't make himself turn the key in the ignition, so he sat there alone with his thoughts as he recalled everything that had happened today.

Sometimes it helped him understand a case better when he could be alone and go over all the facts again in his mind. He'd certainly been right when he had told himself Cheyenne's story was going to be different from any other he'd ever heard. The only other stalker case he remembered working on was a few years ago.

That one had involved a high school girl whose ex-boyfriend wouldn't leave her alone. Her parents had become worried because he seemed to follow her everywhere and had filed a complaint. All it had taken in that case was a talk with the boy's parents, and they had gotten counseling for their son right away. The stalking had stopped, and now both students were off at college in different parts of the country. According to their parents, both of them were doing well.

Cheyenne's case wasn't going to be that easy to deal with, though. She had no idea who her stalker was, and he'd escalated his violence considerably in the time he'd been harassing her. Luke had listened carefully as she'd told her story, but he had the feeling that there was something she wasn't telling him. Call it gut reaction, but whatever it was had proven beneficial in the past.

Then there was the troubling thought about Virgil's cut hand. Had he really injured it opening a hay bale, or had his knife slipped when he was cutting Cheyenne's drag strap?

He reached for the ignition but let his fingers hover over it.

He couldn't get past his doubts about the security guard. He seemed more interested in flirting with a pretty nurse than he did guarding a patient who'd been almost killed. Perhaps he needed to go back and check on him just to see if he was attending to his duty or not.

Before he could change his mind, Luke got out of the truck and headed back inside. He was being ridiculous, but he'd learned long ago not to dismiss those doubts when they took hold in his mind. It wouldn't take but a few minutes to make sure the guard was on task, and if he wasn't, Luke was going to read him the riot act whether it strained relations between the sheriff's office and the hospital or not.

He strode through the doors to the emergency room and was so intent on his mission that he was at the elevator before he realized he hadn't acknowledged the receptionist he'd just hurried past. He'd have to apologize when he came back down.

The doors to the elevator opened and he stepped inside. He hesitated for a moment and considered leaving, and then that feeling hit him again. With a quick jab his finger punched the button for the second floor and the elevator doors closed.

Cheyenne struggled with her attacker and tried to twist free of his grip, but he was too strong. He gave a soft chuckle and pulled her tighter. "You're not getting away from me this time," he whispered.

He pushed her face first against the vending machine, then pulled his arm around her chest. Cheyenne took a quick breath at the relief, but that turned quickly to fear when she realized he'd only released her long enough to pull a knife from his pocket. It was now pressed against the side of her neck, and her breath froze in her throat.

"I have you now, Sunshine," he said. "We're going to leave here. Don't make a sound as we go down the stairs, or I'll kill you where you stand. Do you hear me?"

She gave a slight nod.

"Good girl," he said.

Cheyenne knew he intended to kill her. It didn't matter if he did it here or somewhere else. She had nothing to lose. So although she was trembling with fear, she had to do something.

With the knife still at her throat, he relaxed his fingers on her mouth, and she knew this was her only opportunity. In a moment she would either be free or lying on the floor bleeding to death. She made her decision and sank her teeth in one of his fingers with all her strength.

Crying out in pain, he stumbled backward. When she felt the pressure of the knife ease on her neck, she screamed as loud as she could and pushed away from him. Still screaming at the top of her voice, she ran toward the bathroom in hopes of locking herself inside. She'd just reached the door when his hand clamped around her wrist and he spun her around.

For the first time she saw his face. She'd known when he moved his head to whisper in her ear that he had some kind of mask on, and now she cringed at the sight. He wore a black ski mask, and his wild stare blazed with fury through the eye slits.

"You'll pay for that," he growled as he raised the knife to attack.

"No," she begged as she cowered against the bathroom door.

Suddenly she heard someone run into the room and come to a stop. "Hold it right there!" a loud voice demanded.

She turned to look, and she saw the security guard standing a few feet away with his gun drawn. "Drop the knife and step away from her," he ordered.

Jesse's hands released her, and he did as the guard said. He bent his knees and lowered the knife toward the floor. Then suddenly he charged toward the guard, and Cheyenne watched in horror as he sank the knife into the young man's stomach.

* * *

A scream pierced the quiet of the hospital as Luke stepped off the elevator. The sound sent a jolt of fear through him, and he reached for his gun before he realized he was off duty. His gun was lying on the closet shelf back at his house.

The scream came again, and he bolted down the hall. Two nurses stood beside their station staring down the hall. In a glance he took in the empty chair outside Cheyenne's room and burst through the door. She was nowhere in sight.

The nurses looked around as he ran back into the hall. "What's going on?" he demanded. "Where is Cheyenne?"

The frightened looks on their faces told him that something bad had just happened. One of them pointed toward the end of the hallway. "We heard a scream. Mike, the security guard, has gone to check it out."

Luke was running in the direction they pointed before she had the words out of her mouth. He rounded the corner and stopped at the entrance to the vending room. In the dim light he could see a dark figure holding a frightened Cheyenne, a knife at her throat. On the floor the security guard lay in a pool of blood.

"Back off, Deputy," the hooded figure holding Cheyenne ordered. "I'll kill her if you take another step."

Luke swallowed and let his gaze travel over Cheyenne. She was terrified, and anger rushed through him. He started toward them, but the man stuck the knife closer to her, and Luke stopped. "Okay. Just take it easy. There's no need to panic. Let her go and we can end all this right now. We don't want someone else to get killed."

"It's never going to end for me," he growled. "After what she did to me, she doesn't deserve to live."

"You don't mean that," Luke said as he inched closer.

The man tightened his arm around Cheyenne. "Step away. We're leaving now. If you try to stop us, I'll kill her."

Luke debated his options. He didn't have a weapon, and the guy had a knife at Cheyenne's throat. He'd killed once, and he didn't sound as if he'd hesitate to do it again. He wasn't going to disarm him here without getting one of them killed, so he did the only thing he could think of at the time.

He stepped away from the door.

"Just don't hurt her," he said.

The man chuckled and pulled Cheyenne toward the exit. "I thought you'd see it my way."

Cheyenne cast him a desperate look as she was dragged from the room. The moment they were out of sight, Luke grabbed the gun the security guard had dropped on the floor and ran into the hall. The nurses still stood at the other end. "There's a man hurt in here. Help him and call 911. Tell them an officer needs backup in the parking lot behind the hospital."

Without waiting to see if they did as he ordered, he rushed toward the exit door and down the stairway that led outside. He prayed he wouldn't be too late to save Cheyenne.

SEVEN

Cheyenne struggled to keep her footing as Jesse herded her down the stairs. They'd just rounded the landing that led to the final flight when her shoe scraped the edge of the step, and her foot slipped out from under her. She lurched forward and knew she was going to fall. Jesse tried to tighten his hold on her, but it was too late.

A sharp sting from the knife slicing across the side of her neck made her cry out as she slipped from his grasp and tumbled headfirst down the stairs. Free of his hold, she put her hands out in front of her and tried to brace for the fall that was about to come.

She landed on the concrete floor at the bottom of the steps with a thud and gasped for breath. Jesse's footsteps echoed in the corridor, and she knew he was coming down the stairs toward her. She needed to get up and run, but she couldn't move. The fall had jarred every bone in her body, and they cried out in protest. The cut on her neck only added to the agony.

"Get up!" Jesse screamed as he arrived at her side. Before she could respond, he had grabbed her arm and tugged. "Get up!" he yelled again.

She pushed up on her hands and knees just as she heard the door at the top of the stairs open. Heavy footsteps pounded on the steps. She looked over her shoulder just as Luke reached the landing above. He held a gun, and he had it pointed at Jesse.

"Get away from her!" Luke shouted.

In answer to Luke's demand, Jesse jerked her to her feet and whirled her in front of him. An evil laugh escaped his throat, and he began to back toward the door with her as a shield. "Don't come closer, Conrad!" he shouted. "I'll kill her if you do."

Luke shook his head. "There's no escape for you. Officers are on their way, so it'll go better for you if you give yourself up."

"You're lying," Jesse snarled as he continued to back toward the door.

With the gun still aimed at her captor, Luke eased the rest of the way down the stairs. "They'll be here any minute."

Jesse came to a stop and released his hold on her to reach behind him and open the door. When it swung open, she heard the sound of sirens in the distance coming closer.

"Hear that," Luke said. "It's all over. Let Cheyenne go."

She could feel Jesse's body grow stiff, and his chest began to rise and fall with heavy breaths. Luke stepped closer, and she felt the knife press against her throat again. Then suddenly Jesse's hold on her was gone, and before she could move, he had shoved her into Luke. He wasn't expecting the blow her weight delivered, and he stumbled backward. His arms wrapped around her as he struggled to regain his balance.

Behind them she heard the door close. She looked over her shoulder, and Jesse was gone. "Are you all right, Cheyenne?" Luke's worried voice brought her back to the fact that she was safe, and she turned her head to face him.

All she could do was nod.

He placed his hands on her arms and guided her to sit on the bottom step. "I'm going after him. Stay here and wait for me."

Again she nodded. And then he was gone.

She wrapped her arms around her waist and leaned forward with her head touching her knees and began to cry. She didn't know how long she sat there before she heard the door open again, and she jerked her head in alarm. Luke, not Jesse, walked over to where she sat.

He knelt on the floor and stared into her eyes. "It's okay now."

"D-did you catch him?" she stammered.

He shook his head. "No, he disappeared in the shadows. I heard a truck start over on the next street, but by the time I got there, he was gone. We have a BOLO out on a dark colored pickup, but that could be any one of a hundred trucks in this town. I'm afraid he's gotten away."

She bowed her head and bit down on her lip as her body shook. After a moment she looked up into his eyes. "If it wasn't for you, I'd be dead now." She was still sitting on the bottom step with her hands clasped in her lap, and he covered them with his. The warmth from his fingers had a calming effect on her. "Thank you for what you did."

He swallowed hard. "I'm just glad I came back."

With a start she sat up straighter, her eyes wide. "The security guard. Jesse stabbed him."

Too late she realized what she'd said, and then Luke asked the question she'd known he would. "Jesse? He has a name? You didn't tell me that."

"I—I don't know if that's his real name or not."

Luke exhaled a deep breath and pushed to his feet. Her heart quaked at the stern look he directed down at her.

"Cheyenne, is there something you haven't told me about your stalker?"

She laced her fingers together and twisted them. "I haven't told anyone," she whispered.

The serious expression on his face dissolved and was replaced by a kind one, and his eyes softened. "I can't help you if I don't know the whole story," he said.

Her breath hitched in her throat, and she shook her head. "I—I can't. I'm too embarrassed."

He clasped her hands in his and pulled her

to her feet. His gaze traveled over her face, and she felt her pulse quicken. He gave her hands a squeeze and leaned closer. "Cheyenne, I will listen to whatever you have to say. Then I will help you to make things right. You deserve to find some peace. Please give me the chance to make that happen. You can trust me."

She looked into his eyes and suddenly she knew. For the first time since this whole nightmare started, she had finally found someone she truly believed could help her—that she could trust. It was time to tell the truth to someone, and Luke Conrad was that person.

Luke couldn't hear the sirens anymore, and he glanced back at the exit door. "Wait here while I check and see if our guys were able to catch him."

He opened the door and stepped out into the dark night just as two sheriff's cars pulled into the parking lot, their blue lights blinking. They came to a stop, and Luke walked toward them. As he approached the vehicles, Sheriff Ben Whitman stepped out from one of them and headed toward Luke.

"Ben," he called out. "I thought you were still out of town."

"I got back a few hours ago, just in time to find out that it had been quite a night at the Wild West show." The sheriff came to a stop beside Luke and pulled on the brim of his cowboy hat so that it settled farther down on his forehead.

Luke nodded. "Yeah, and now whoever tried to kill Cheyenne has tried it again. Did he get away?"

"I'm afraid so."

Luke exhaled and shook his head. "This guy's had a busy night. He sabotaged Cheyenne's equipment, and then he tried to kill her. The hospital security guard who tried to help her ended up stabbed. I need to get inside and check on him."

Ben regarded him with a quizzical expression for a moment before his mouth curled into a grin. "Cheyenne? I don't think I've ever heard you call a female victim by her first name. I expected it to be Miss Cassidy. Interesting."

"Cut it out, Ben," Luke growled. "She's had a rough time today, and we've been together a lot."

"That's what I heard," Ben said, his eyes twinkling in the light coming from the cars.

"What do you mean you heard? Who've you been talking to?"

Ben tilted his head to one side. "Dean filled me in on the day's events."

"That's right," Luke said. "I forgot you and Dean are best friends."

Ben nodded. "Yes, and I met Cheyenne right after she came to town when Dean and Gwen invited me to dinner. She told me her story because the media was still keeping up with what was happening in her life and how she'd coped with her tragedy. Do you think what happened today has anything to do with that case?"

For the next few minutes, Luke filled in Ben on all the information that Cheyenne had given him earlier today. When he'd finished, he shook his head. "But there's more I need to find out."

"What's that?"

"When she was recounting her story today, she never indicated that she knew her stalker's name, but after this incident tonight, she called him Jesse. There's something she's not telling me, and I intend to find out what it is."

Ben nodded. "I'm sure if anybody can win her trust, it's you. You've made a great officer, Luke. I know your dad would have been so proud to see how far you've come."

At the mention of his father, Luke swallowed hard and tried to keep an impassive expression on his face. "Thanks, Ben. I wish he could have seen it."

Ben nodded and slapped him on the back. "Let's go inside and check on the security guard and Cheyenne."

Together they walked into the hospital. Cheyenne was still sitting on the steps where he'd left her. When the door opened, she looked up with a scared look on her face and jumped to her feet. "Did they catch him?"

Luke shook his head. "I'm sorry."

She glanced at Ben. "Sheriff Whitman? I didn't expect to see you here."

"I just got back into town. I understand you've had a rough day. Are you okay now?"

She looked at Luke, and his heart squeezed at the way her eyes stared into his. "I am thanks to Luke. I don't know what I would have done today without his help."

He took a deep breath as his heartbeat increased at her words. He stepped closer and took her by the arm. "And we need to get you back to your room."

"And I need to check on the security guard," Ben added.

Luke loosened his grip on Cheyenne's arm as he guided her back up the steps with Ben following. When they arrived at the vending machine room, one of the housekeeping employees rounded the corner. He was pushing a cart with cleaning supplies. Ben came to a halt and put up a hand to stop the man.

"We can't have this room cleaned. It's a crime scene. I'm going to close it off so no one will come in here. We'll let you know when you can get in here, but it won't be tonight."

The man frowned. "Okay. I was just trying to do my job."

"I understand," Ben said. "We'll let you know."

As he turned around and headed back the way he had come, Ben glanced at Luke. "Get Cheyenne settled, and I'll make arrangements for this to be taken care of."

Luke gave a chin lift in Ben's direction before he nudged Cheyenne down the hallway toward her room. As they walked away, he could hear Ben on his lapel mic asking for officers to come to the vending room to put up crime scene tape and for the crime scene investigators to be called in.

The two nurses Luke had seen earlier stood in the hallway next to their station as they approached. "We've been worried about you two. We called the police like you asked. Did they get there in time?"

Luke shook his head. "They weren't able to catch the guy who stabbed the guard. How is he doing?"

The other nurse spoke up. "They rushed him to surgery. We haven't heard anything yet, but we'll let you know when we do. I called the head of security, and he's coming in to guard Miss Cassidy's door himself."

"Good. I'll stay until he gets here," Luke said.

The first nurse stepped closer to Cheyenne. "Let's get you settled, and I'll check you out to make sure you're okay." She glanced back at Luke. "Give us a few minutes, please."

Luke's gaze went to Cheyenne, and he pointed to the chair where the guard had been sitting. "I'll be right here."

She nodded and went into the room with the nurse as he took a seat. Ten minutes later the nurse emerged. "She's all settled."

"How is she?"

"Blood pressure was up, but that's to be expected after what she experienced tonight. Now she just needs to get some rest."

"I'll step in and tell her good-night, then I'll wait out here for the guard," he said.

He opened the door, stepped into the room and stopped beside the bed. She lay with her head slightly raised, and her hair spread out on her pillow. Her brown eyes sparkled in the soft light of the room.

Jasmine's eyes had been brown, too, but there'd been too many lies hidden in their depths. Cheyenne Cassidy had a secret, too, and he intended to find out what it was.

He cleared his throat before he spoke. "How are you?" he asked.

She smiled up at him. "I'm okay, thanks to you. I thought he was going to be successful this time. Then you appeared, and I just knew everything was going to be all right."

"I'm just glad I got there in time."

She smiled, and the way her mouth curled made his breath hitch in his throat. He shook the thought from his head, pulled a chair up to her bed and sat down so that he wasn't towering over her but could stare into her face. "I think there's something we need to discuss. I don't like bringing it up, especially after what you've gone through tonight, but it's important if we are to catch this guy."

Her eyes darkened and she frowned. "What is it?"

"When you were giving me your statement today, you led me to believe you didn't know your stalker. Tonight you called him Jesse, and you said you didn't tell me because you were embarrassed. I don't understand."

Her hands gripped the sheet, and she began to pleat it between her trembling fingers. "As I said, I haven't told anybody." Her voice shook and her eyes filled with tears. "But I should have. Maybe if I had, my parents would still be alive."

Luke scooted to the edge of his chair and directed a somber stare at her. "Cheyenne, you need to be honest with me if I'm going to help you. I can't if you're keeping me in the dark about something that may be a clue as to these attempts on your life."

She looked at her hands. "I was lonely," she finally whispered.

When she didn't say anything else, he leaned closer. "And?"

"I was home from college, but nothing was the same. All my friends I'd grown up with had moved away or were married with families. My college friends had fanned out all across the country, and I didn't have anybody. One night I was alone at home, my folks had gone to a horse sale and were going to be gone all night. I got on the computer, and next thing I knew I had searched out and joined an online chat room."

She bit down on her lip, and was silent again. After a moment she took a deep breath and continued. "Nobody listed their real names. So I called myself Patches."

He smiled. "After your horse."

She nodded. "I began to chat, and there was this one person who seemed to have the same interests as me. We both liked horses, and he asked me if I would like to make our messages private so we could talk about what we wanted. I agreed, and so that's how it began. After that we talked every night, sometimes for hours. He told me he grew up in West Virginia on a farm, and he had ridden horses all his life. He said he was living in Massachusetts now and working as an accountant."

"And he told you his real name?"

"He said it was Jesse Tolliver and that he worked for the accounting firm of Morris, Templeton and Bradford in Boston."

"Did you ever check him out to see if there really was a Jesse Tolliver?"

"I did. I looked up the accounting firm, and they had an accountant by that name."

"Did you ever see a picture of him?"

"Yes, he sent me a picture that he said was of him."

"What happened next?" Luke asked.

Cheyenne pulled one of her hands free of his grip and rubbed it across her forehead. "We talked every night for several months, and then the tone of his messages began to change. I had thought of Jesse as a friend who was lonely like me, so one night I told him about this new guy I'd met and was going out on a date with. He got angry and told me I couldn't go, that he was the only man I could have in my life. I tried to reason with him, but it was no use. The things he said scared me, and so I quit connecting with him."

"But that wasn't the end of it?"

Cheyenne shook her head. "No. I had been stupid enough to give him all my information. He knew where I lived, my telephone number, my email and that I performed in rodeos. That's when the texts and the letters started coming. The messages usually related what I'd done that day or what I'd worn. When he threatened to kill my boyfriend, I broke up with him. Then came the worst thing of all."

She paused, and a sob ripped from her throat. Luke grasped her hand tighter and leaned closer. "What was the worst thing?"

She bit down on her lip for a moment before she answered. Then she took a deep breath. "He told me he was giving me one more chance. If I wanted to make right what I'd done to him, I would meet him at the next rodeo where I was scheduled to ride. I was so scared that I didn't go. I stayed home."

Understanding began to dawn on Luke, but he figured she had to say the words that she'd held in for so long. "Go on."

"My parents went without me, and he killed them." She shuddered and closed her eyes for a moment before she opened them and stared up at him. A tear rolled down her face, and she gave a little hiccup before she spoke. "I should have told my parents or the police about Jesse, but I was too embarrassed to let them know how stupid I was. At first I thought he'd grow tired and leave me alone. As time went on, it got worse, and he threatened to do horrible things to me if I told anybody his name. So I kept quiet, and my parents died."

"Cheyenne, you didn't—" he began.

"No," she interrupted. "There's nothing you can say that will change my mind. I'm responsible for my parents' murder, and I have to live with that knowledge for the rest of my life."

EIGHT

Cheyenne lay back on the pillows and closed her eyes. Finally she'd told someone, and it felt like a huge weight had been lifted. It didn't change the fact that she still believed she was responsible for her parents' deaths, but at least now someone else knew. The only problem was that it had been Luke who learned the truth about her.

There was something about him that she'd liked the minute she looked up and saw him bending over her earlier today when she'd run into his car. Since that time, he'd demonstrated over and over the kindness he possessed. She'd hoped that he would be the first friend she'd make outside of the Johnsons and the Harwells. Now he probably saw her for the secretive, deceitful daughter she'd been and would want nothing to do with her.

She opened her eyes and stared up at Luke, and her breath hitched in her throat. He wasn't frowning, as she suspected he would be. Instead he stared at her with a sad look in his eyes and nodded. "It's not easy waking up every day filled with remorse. I should know. I've been doing it for years."

"What do you mean?"

Luke took a deep breath and stared down at the floor for a moment before he answered. "My dad was the greatest man I've ever known. When I was little, I wanted to be with him all the time. I followed him everywhere, and I knew that when I grew up I wanted to be just like him. My mother had died when I was young, so it was just the two of us, and his world revolved around me."

"That sounds a lot like the relationship I had with my dad except I had my mother, too," she said.

Luke pursed his lips for a moment before he continued. "When I got older, I began to change. I thought he was too strict, and all I wanted to do was get out on my own. I went to college for a few years, but I didn't really like it, so I enlisted in the army. By the time I came home, I'd been in combat and thought I was a real tough guy. One night I'd been drinking at a bar and got in an argument with a man who tried to hit on the girl I was with. We ended up in a fight, and we both were arrested. I called my dad from the jail, and he said he'd come bail me out. I knew it was late, and I knew it was raining, but I wanted to go home. So I told him to come. On the way he skidded on the wet road and hit a tree. He didn't die. He lived for six months in a coma, and I had to watch the life slowly drain out of him because of what I'd done."

Cheyenne scooted up in the bed. "Oh, no!"

"So you see, I know what it's like to feel responsible."

"I guess you do, but you couldn't help that his car hit a tree."

"Just as you couldn't help it because your stalker made the decision to kill your parents."

Cheyenne thought for a moment about what he'd said, then sighed and shook her head. "It's a terrible thing to live with guilt. Tell me how you do it."

He sighed and raked his hand through his hair. "Ben helped me see that I didn't have to. He had just been elected sheriff, and we'd been friends a long time. He knew what I was going through, and he came out to the ranch I'd inherited one night. He talked to me about how much my dad loved me and said that he wouldn't want me to blame myself."

"But you did,," Cheyenne interrupted. "Just like I do."

Luke nodded. "Yeah. Getting rid of guilt is easier said than done. But Ben reminded me that God forgives our sins all the time, and He's our father. So if God can forgive, then my dad would have forgiven me, too."

The memory of standing at her parents' graves returned, and she felt fresh tears in her eyes. "Our pastor said much the same thing to me after my parents' deaths, and I know they'd forgive me for not telling them. The problem is I can't forget what happened."

Luke paused for a moment before he spoke. "When I was about ten years old, I opened my mother's jewelry box even though my father had warned me to leave it alone. Everything in it reminded him of her, and he didn't want anything to happen to the things that she had loved. I took out her locket that I knew he gave her before they were married and put it in my pocket. At the end of the day when I went to put it back, it was gone. I don't know where I lost, but I couldn't find it anywhere."

Cheyenne's eyes grew wide. "What did your father do when he found out?"

Luke chuckled. "Of course he was furious. He punished me by taking away all television for a month, and he gave me extra chores around the ranch to keep me busy. I took my punishment, and then he told me that he'd forgiven me for disobeying him and that we would never talk about it again. I know he didn't forget because he loved my mother, and he treasured that locket, but he chose not to remember it because he loved me, too. That's what I had to do. I had to realize that Dad would have forgiven me for asking him to come, and he would never have reminded me of it again."

"And that's helped you live with it?"

"It has," Luke said. "I haven't forgotten what happened, but I choose not to remember it with guilt. I asked God's forgiveness, and I have it. So I know I have my father's forgiveness also."

Tears came into Cheyenne's eyes again. "You make it sound so easy."

"Oh, no," he said. "It's not easy. It's one of the hardest things I've ever done, but I decided it wasn't going to rule my life. I was going to make something of myself to make my dad proud. I went to Ben and asked him if he would consider making me a deputy sheriff. The charges against me had been dropped, and I didn't have a record, so he agreed. I've worked hard to be the best officer I can be, and I know my dad would be proud of me."

Cheyenne let her gaze drift over him. "I think he would be, too."

Luke started to respond, but before he could there was a knock at the door. A man stuck his head inside and looked toward Luke. "Sorry to interrupt, Luke."

Luke got from the chair and motioned for the man to come into the room. "That's okay, Jeff. I wondered if you were going to come."

The man stopped beside her bed and looked down at Cheyenne. "Miss Cassidy, my name is Jeff Swan. I'm the head of security here at the hospital, and I'm very sorry about what you've had to go through tonight."

"How's the guard who was stabbed?" Luke asked.

"He's still in surgery. Maybe we'll know something before long."

Luke put his hands in his pockets and rocked

back on his heels. "How long has he been working for you?"

"Not long, but he went through our training program. The nurses at the desk told me he seemed more interested in flirting with them tonight than he did with doing his job."

Luke arched an eyebrow. "Well…"

Jeff glanced at Cheyenne. "Don't you worry, Miss Cassidy. I'll be right outside your door for the rest of the night. Nothing else is going to happen to you." He turned back to Luke. "I'm sorry it took me so long to get here, but I'm ready to take over if you want to go on home."

"I think I'll do that. I'll just say good-night to Cheyenne, then I'll be on my way."

"Then I'll see you when you leave," Jeff said. "Miss Cassidy, if you need anything at all, don't hesitate to call either the nurse or me."

"Thank you, Mr. Swan. I'll do that."

With a nod in their direction he turned and walked out the door. When it closed behind him, Luke looked back at her. "I'll come in the morning and check on you. If you're still doing well and the doctor dismisses you, I'll take you home."

The expectant look he directed at her seemed

to indicate he was asking permission to come back. She started to object, to say that Gwen could come, but for some reason she wanted Luke to be the one. So she smiled as she stared up at him. "I'd like that. I'll be waiting for you."

His Adam's apple bobbed as he swallowed, and a slight flush tinged his cheeks. "See you then." He headed to the door but stopped and faced her again. "When I take you home tomorrow, I'd like to get your computer and take it with me. We have some tech guys who do great work. They might be able to track all the messages you exchanged with Jesse and discover who he really is."

Cheyenne frowned. "I don't think they'll be able to. I deleted all the messages."

"That doesn't matter. Nothing is ever completely lost. If anything's still there, they'll find it."

Her eyes grew large. "Do you really think they might be able to locate him?"

Luke shrugged. "I don't know, but it's worth a try."

"It seems like you just keep giving me reasons to thank you."

He smiled down at her. "It's my job, but in

your case, it's also a pleasure. Anything I can get for you before I leave?"

"No. You've done quite a lot tonight. I'll never forget it, Luke."

He gave a slight nod. "So I'll see you tomorrow," he said as he walked away. Cheyenne sat without moving and stared at his retreating figure as he headed to the door. When he put his hand on the doorknob, he paused and looked back over his shoulder. "Sweet dreams, Cheyenne."

Before she could answer, he was out the door, and it was closing softly behind him. She lay back against the pillows and smiled. It had been a long day, and she was tired. She'd had two attempts on her life and a man guarding her had been hurt. The ordeal had left her drained of energy, but she doubted if she would be able to go to sleep.

She closed her eyes as Luke's voice and his soft spoken words played over and over in her head. *Sweet dreams,* he'd said. The soothing effect made her yawn and she snuggled down under the covers. Maybe Luke wanted to be her friend after all. She hoped so. In the short time she'd known him, she had come to recognize he was a good man, a kind one she was sure her parents would have liked.

With that thought in mind, she felt herself growing drowsy. *Sweet dreams.* The words echoed in her head one last time before she drifted into a deep sleep.

A week later Luke walked out of the new barn at Little Pigeon Ranch. He couldn't help but remember the night a year ago when Dean's old barn had burned down. Thankfully all the horses had been saved, and now a new state-of-the-art structure occupied the space where the old one had sat. The horses on Little Pigeon should feel fortunate to have such grand quarters to live in. He only wished he could afford something like this. Maybe someday when he was able to get his horse-breeding business off the ground. At the present time, however, that seemed a long way off. He didn't have the capital to get the venture going or a partner to help him run it.

He dismissed the thoughts and had just stepped outside the double doors as Dean rode up on his horse, Midnight. Luke waited for his friend to dismount, then approached him.

"Hey, Dean. Where've you been?"

Dean held Midnight's reins in his hand and led the horse toward the barn. "I rode over to the back of the ranch to check on the fences. Everything seemed okay. What are you doing here again?" he asked with a sly smile.

Luke's eyebrows arched, and he stared at Dean. "I wanted to see if Cheyenne had heard anything from her stalker, but she said he's been quiet all week."

"Yeah," Dean said. "We've all been on alert around here in case he shows up, but so far nothing. Have you talked to her yet?"

"I have. I thought while I was here I would help with Patches's therapy. I've been worried about the horse."

Dean couldn't hide the grin on his face. "It just seems like you've been over here about every day this week. I just wondered if you were really coming to see Patches or the girl who rides him."

Luke felt his face grow warm, and he scowled. "Cut it out, Dean. I like Cheyenne, and I'm sorry about what happened to her horse. She's had a rough time the past few years, and I just want to make things better for her. You know I'm not looking for a relationship, not after what happened with Jasmine."

"Not all women are like your ex," Dean said.

Luke nodded. "I know that, but it's made me stop and think before I risk getting involved with anyone again."

Dean pursed his lips and clamped his hand on Luke's shoulder. "I understand. In any case I'm glad you're coming around. Cheyenne needs some friends. Gwen and I have tried to be that for her, but a woman like her needs to spend time with people her own age." Dean's eyes searched Luke's face. "Someone like you."

Luke swallowed and tried to ignore the way his pulse quickened. "I like her, Dean. I'm enjoying getting to know her."

"Good." Dean took a deep breath. "So how's the investigation going? The tech guys found anything on her computer?"

"Not yet, but they're still working. I was right about the phone, though. It was a burner. They said they'd let me know as soon as they found anything."

Dean sighed. "Well, as a former cop, I know a case isn't solved in a single day. It takes time."

"You got that right."

"How's the hospital guard who was stabbed doing?"

"Better. I talked with the doctor this morning, and they've moved him out of the intensive care unit into a room. Ben went over to question him, but the guy couldn't tell him anything. Of course, the attacker had on a ski mask, and there was very little light in the room so he couldn't make out any details."

"That's too bad," Dean murmured. He started to say more, but at that moment Cheyenne came out of the barn. She held a bucket in her hand and was laughing with Maggie, who walked along beside her. They were almost to where Luke and Dean stood before she looked up and saw them there.

Maggie spotted her dad at that same moment and gave a little shriek as she ran toward him. "Daddy!" she cried. "You left before I got up this morning. I wanted to go with you."

Dean reached down with one arm and scooped up his daughter. She wrapped her arms around his neck and, smiling, leaned forward for the two of them to rub noses. Dean laughed and stared into her eyes. "You didn't need to go this time, darling. You'd have been tired out, but we can take a short ride this afternoon if you want."

Maggie frowned and looked at her father. "We have to be back in time to help Mommy decorate the Christmas tree."

"Oh, we'll be back way before that. We won't start on the tree until after dinner."

Maggie twisted around in her father's arms and stared at Luke. "Do you have your tree up yet, Luke?" she asked.

Luke chuckled and shook his head. "No. I don't have one."

Maggie's mouth dropped open, as if she'd never heard anything so ridiculous in her life. "Why not? Don't you like Christmas?"

"Of course I do, but I'm a man living alone. Most bachelors don't bother to put up a tree."

"Bother?" Maggie's whispered word made him suddenly feel like he was Scrooge in the flesh, and he glanced at Cheyenne, who was trying to hide her smile with her hand. "If you don't have a Christmas tree, Luke," Maggie continued, "you have to share ours."

He started to refuse, but Dean spoke up first. "I think that's a great idea, Maggie. Luke needs to help us decorate so he can get in the

Christmas spirit." He glanced at Luke. "How about coming to dinner tonight and helping us put up the tree?"

"Uh, I don't know," he muttered and looked at Cheyenne, who seemed to be waiting for him to say something. "Do you want me to come?" he asked.

She smiled and nodded. "Very much. I think it will be a lot of fun."

The way her eyes sparkled sent a thrill through him, and he smiled back. "Then I'll be here. What time is dinner?"

Dean headed toward the barn with Maggie on one arm as he led Midnight with the other. "Be here about six thirty," he called over his shoulder. "It'll be good to have another guy around to keep the women from getting too carried away with the decorations."

"Oh, Daddy," Maggie said as they left, "you know you like to help decorate."

"I like anything I get to do with you, darling," Dean said before he and his daughter entered the barn.

Luke suddenly felt shy being left alone with Cheyenne. Just minutes before they had been talking, but that had been about Patches. Now there was no horse to discuss, just the fact that he was coming back for a dinner that was usually reserved for family.

"It's been a long while since I helped decorate a Christmas tree," he said.

A sad look flashed in her eyes. "My family used to do it every year. My father would always cut one that had grown on the ranch and bring it in and get it set up. Then after dinner the three of us would gather in the den and put on the decorations that my mother had collected all the Christmases since they'd been married. I'm sure you must have some memories from your childhood."

Luke smiled. "I remember the last Christmas my mother was alive. She was sick, but she insisted that we have a wonderful Christmas. She did everything she could to make it that way. Sometimes I think I can still smell the cookies that she baked, and I remember what the tree looked like. It had twinkling lights, all colors of balls and a big star on the top. She hung every construction-paper and Popsicle-stick ornament I'd ever made in school on it and said it was a special tree for her Luke. Then on Christmas morning the three of us sat beside it before we opened presents, while she read the story of Christ's birth from the book of Luke. When she finished, she told me she'd always loved that story and named me after that book in the Bible."

Cheyenne had stepped closer to him and laid her hand on his arm. "That sounds like a wonderful memory."

He nodded. "It was the best Christmas I ever had."

She smiled and squeezed his arm. "Maybe we can help make this a good Christmas for each other."

He swallowed. "I hope so." He could tell she was about to say something else when her cell phone chimed for an incoming text. "Excuse me. I need to see who this is."

She pulled it from her pocket and opened the message. Suddenly her face paled, and she closed her eyes. Luke reached out and grabbed her arm. "What's wrong?"

"He hasn't gotten in touch with me since the night Patches and I fell. Now it starts again."

Luke jerked the phone from her hand and stared down at the message. I don't like Luke Conrad spending so much time with you. Tell him to leave now and stay away if you want him to live.

He looked back at Cheyenne, and she had

her fist jammed against her lips. Her eyes were large and terror-filled. "He wants to kill anybody he thinks I'm becoming close to. What are we going to do?"

Luke had no idea, but he couldn't tell her that. At the moment all he could think about was how her stalker knew they had spent time together for the past week. He turned his head and scanned the area as far as he could see, but he couldn't make out anybody watching them.

A cold chill went up his spine. Somebody knew he was here, so whoever it was had to have seen them. But where was he? Now instead of just watching out for Cheyenne he had to worry about himself, too. He hoped those tech guys could find something soon before someone else was hurt—or killed. And if that text was true, it looked like he might be the next intended victim.

NINE

Cheyenne stood next to Luke and watched Maggie put the last ornament on the Christmas tree. Her lips trembled, but she cleared her throat and tried to ignore the roiling in her stomach. She remembered as a little girl putting the final touch to her family's tree, and now she was in someone else's home watching it being done by their child.

Next to her, Luke seemed to sense her moment of nostalgia, and he slipped his fingers around hers. She turned her head to stare at him, and suddenly she didn't feel quite so sad anymore. His smile lit his blue eyes, and she studied his face for a moment before she returned the gesture.

The feeling she'd had a few minutes ago seemed to dissipate as she laced her fingers with his and grasped them tighter just as she heard Maggie laugh and clap her hands. Cheyenne turned her head to see what was so funny and saw that Dean had plugged in the twinkling lights. The tree was now ablaze, and Maggie's eyes were filled with wonder.

The little girl looked over her shoulder, and her shrill voice echoed in the room. "Cheyenne, isn't this the most beautiful tree you've ever seen?"

All Cheyenne could do was nod because her heart had filled with a new sensation she hadn't felt in several years. She looked around at Luke, Dean, Gwen and Maggie, and knew she wasn't really alone in the world. They'd all invited her into their lives and made her feel welcome. She hadn't expected to ever find that again.

She smiled at Maggie and finally found her voice. "I think you're right. It is the most beautiful tree I've ever seen." She glanced at Luke. "What do you think?"

He smiled, but his gaze wasn't on the tree. It remained on her. "Beautiful," he whispered, and Cheyenne felt her heart race.

She didn't know what to say, so she was relieved when Gwen spoke up. "Okay, it's time for hot cocoa, and then it's off to bed for Maggie." She glanced at Dean and her daughter. "I need you two to help me in the kitchen."

"Anything you say," Dean said as he grinned and followed his wife from the room.

Luke glanced at Cheyenne and shook his head. "Do you get the feeling that we've just been set up?"

Cheyenne pursed her lips and nodded. "I think you're right." She tilted her head and looked up at him. "So what do you think we should do?"

"I think we should sit down on the couch and take in the beauty of that Christmas tree," he said.

Still holding his hand, Cheyenne turned and led him to the sofa. When they were settled, she glanced around the room. The fire that Gwen had lit, along with candles that burned on several tables and the twinkling Christmas tree, produced a peaceful atmosphere, and she sighed in pleasure. "This is nice," she said.

"It is," Luke agreed. "I'd forgotten how special something like putting lights on a tree can be. I'm glad I got to see Maggie having such a good time tonight. Christmas is really a special season for children."

"It is. I was worried that this Christmas was

going to be difficult because it's the first one without my parents, but I realized tonight how blessed I've been. I get to spend it with new friends in a new place." She swiveled in the seat until she faced him. "What have you done on Christmas since your father died?"

Luke shrugged. "I work. Since so many of the other deputies have families, I always volunteer to take the holiday shifts. That way Ben can work it out so that they can all be with their families at some time during the day."

Cheyenne's heart pricked at his words. She'd never thought about those whose jobs were geared to public service having to miss Christmas with their families. The fact that Luke tried to make it better for the people he worked with made her admire him even more than she already did.

"That's very nice of you, Luke."

His face reddened a bit, and he ducked his head as he gave a little chuckle. "Just trying to help out," he said.

"The way you've been doing for me ever since we met. You've gone out of your way to help with Patches, and what has your kindness gotten you? A threat against your life. I'm so sorry about that."

He reached over and covered her hand with his. "I'm used to things like that. I'm in law enforcement. This guy's not the first one who's wanted to kill me."

Her happy mood vanished at his words. "But this time, it's because of me, the same as it was with my parents."

He sat up straight and shook his head. "Don't think that way, Cheyenne. You haven't done anything wrong. Your stalker wants to make you believe it's your fault. That's what they do to victims. You have to remember that he picked you out of all those people in that chat room. You were targeted before you even knew it, and he set about to reel you in. Now we've got to catch him so it doesn't happen to someone else."

Before Cheyenne could respond, Gwen came back into the room carrying a tray with two cups of cocoa on it. She set it on the coffee table in front of the sofa and smiled. "Here's some hot chocolate for you. Maggie manages better at the kitchen table, so Dean and I are going to stay in there with her. Dean and I both have some work to do after we put her to bed, so we'll bid you good-night. Luke, stay as long as you want, and Cheyenne, please turn off the Christmas tree lights before you go to bed."

Cheyenne barely had time to respond before her friend had turned and walked from the room. When she was out of sight, Cheyenne looked at Luke, and they both burst out laughing. "Yep," Cheyenne said. "They're setting us up."

Luke's face flushed, and he chuckled. "Seems like it. I hope you don't mind."

Cheyenne felt her heart thump, and she swallowed her surprise. "I don't mind it at all," she finally whispered.

A sigh of relief escaped Luke's mouth and his lips curled into a smile. "That's very good news," he said. "I think I knew you were someone I wanted to be friends with the minute I saw your shocked face through the windshield of my car."

Cheyenne tilted her head to one side and directed a teasing look at him. "I have to admit I wasn't so sure about you. When a man keeps calling you 'ma'am,' you wonder if he thinks you're ready to be put out to pasture."

Luke laughed. "Not a chance." Suddenly a sober expression crossed his face. "I'm glad you came to the Smokies, Cheyenne."

Her heart was beating in double time now, and she inhaled a deep breath. "So am I," she murmured.

They sat staring into each other's eyes for a moment, and Luke leaned closer. She closed her eyes in anticipation of his lips on hers, but the moment was interrupted when his cell phone rang. She opened her eyes and saw that he was inches away, staring at her.

When the phone rang again, he bit down on his lip and shook his head before he pulled the device from his pocket. "That's the ringtone for the station. I have to answer this."

She nodded. "I understand."

He exhaled and connected the call. "Conrad." He listened for a moment before he darted a quick glance at her, rose and walked out of the room into the hallway.

Cheyenne could hear him speaking softly, but she didn't try to make out what he was saying. She just hoped he wasn't being called to report to the station because they needed his help with some crime that had been committed. She scooted to the edge of the couch, leaned toward the coffee table and picked up her cup of cocoa. As she sipped it, she heard Luke's voice again.

"Thanks, Andy. I appreciate all your work on this. Can you send copies of everything to my email?" He paused for a moment. "Good deal. I'll see you tomorrow."

She took another sip from her cup and looked up as he came back to the couch and sat down. A troubled look lined his face, and it concerned her. She set the cup back on the tray and turned to him. "You look like you've had bad news. Is something wrong?"

He gave a small nod. "That was Andy, one of the tech guys who does work for us at the station. He's the one who's been trying to recover the emails on your computer."

Cheyenne sat up straighter. "Has he had any luck?"

Luke raked his hand through his hair. "Yeah. He has."

When he didn't continue, Cheyenne frowned. "Don't keep me guessing. What did he say?"

"He retrieved all the messages on your computer and has them copied. Then he contacted the accounting firm in Boston where Jesse said he worked. They did have an employee named Jesse Tolliver, but he died nearly four years ago."

Cheyenne's eyes grew large. "What? How did he die?"

"Apparently from natural causes. He had a terminal illness."

Cheyenne's mouth dropped open. "So somebody took his identity and used it to join a chat room?"

"It looks like that."

Cheyenne sat still and mulled over what Luke had just said. She pushed up from the couch, wrapped her arms around her waist and began to pace back and forth across the floor. On her third trip, she stopped and stared at Luke, who had been watching her silently.

"So my stalker is someone who lives in the Boston area and probably knew the real Jesse Tolliver had died?"

Luke got to his feet and came to stand beside her. "I don't know. Anybody can troll the internet for obituaries and assume a name. But Andy doesn't think this guy is from Boston."

"Why not?"

"Because his computer messages are from different towns all across the country. A lot of them are from here, and they're all from public ISPs."

Cheyenne cocked an eyebrow. "Which means...?"

"The messages were sent from a public place, like a restaurant or a hotel, not from an internet provider paid for by someone like a home owner. It's impossible to tell the owners of computers on a public ISP."

"Not at all?"

Luke rubbed the back of his neck. "Well, only if the person sending the messages used that computer at the same public place to log in to one of his personal accounts that has his real name on it, like a bank or a credit card. Something like that would leave a trace."

Cheyenne sighed. "I'm guessing my stalker hasn't done that."

Luke shook his head. "Not that Andy has found, but he's not going to stop looking."

The peaceful feeling that she'd had just minutes ago had left her. Cheyenne felt the fear she'd carried for three years return. She tried to blink the tears from her eyes, but it was no use.

"I'm never going to be free of him," she whispered.

Luke was beside her before the words were out of her mouth and he wrapped his fingers around her arms. "Don't give in to that kind of thinking. We know more now than we did. At least we know the towns he was in when the messages were sent. Andy is sending me all the locations and the dates. We'll go from there."

"Do you think it will help?"

"I don't know, but it's worth a try." A tear slid from her eye and he reached up with his thumb and wiped it away. "Stay strong for me, Cheyenne. We'll catch this guy."

The intense look on his face and the way he spoke the words told her that he intended to do what he said. That was enough to bring a flicker of hope back to her. She nodded as her lips pulled into a wobbly smile. "I know you will, Luke. Thank you for all you're doing for me."

The muscle in his jaw clenched as his grip on her arms tightened. "I want to do more. You've lived with this situation for three years, and it's been an emotional drain on you. I saw you having fun tonight decorating the tree, and now it's ruined. I'm sorry about that."

"I'll be all right. It takes a few minutes for

me to get back to normal after my thoughts return to him. I just need to refocus my mind."

Luke smiled. "I know a great way you can refocus."

"How's that?"

"Have dinner with me tomorrow night. I'm on the day shift, but I'll pick you up after work and introduce you to my favorite restaurant in the Smokies. How about it?"

"Okay." She answered so quickly that it surprised her. She didn't usually make such hasty decisions, but this was a no-brainer. She couldn't think of anything she'd rather do than have dinner with Luke. "That sounds good to me."

The next night Luke sat across the table from Cheyenne and watched as she let her gaze drift over the dining room of the restaurant where he'd eaten so often. This had been his favorite place for years, but tonight it seemed even more special. The atmosphere created by soft music playing over the speakers, the perfection of the food and Cheyenne's company had provided the best evening he'd experienced in a long time.

He picked up his coffee cup and stared at her

over the rim. The candle on the table flickered, and its light reflected in her dark, brown eyes. That was the first thing he'd noticed about her. The eyes. He'd never seen any that had such depth that they looked like deep pools of chocolate, and he couldn't quit looking at them.

She glanced back at him and caught him staring at her. "What is it?" she asked.

He hurriedly dropped his gaze and shook his head. "Nothing. I was just thinking what a good time I've had tonight."

She smiled. "I have, too. Thank you for bringing me here." She picked up her fork, put the last bite of her apple pie in her mouth and groaned with pleasure. "That's so good."

He couldn't help but grin at the look on her face. "Do you need another cup of coffee to finish the dinner off?"

She leaned back in her chair and rubbed her hands over her stomach. "I couldn't hold anything else. This was wonderful, Luke. It's been ages since I had such a good time."

He pushed his dessert plate out of the way and folded his arms on top of the table. "I'm glad. It was my pleasure to see you enjoying the evening."

She reached across and placed her hand on

top of his. "Everything's been great. Especially the company."

His heartbeat increased at her touch, and he felt a tingle in his arm. He looked down at her hand and turned his so that their fingers were laced together. "That goes double for me."

Her eyes twinkled. "Maybe we can do it again."

The teasing tone of her voice made his skin warm, and he tightened his fingers on hers as he leaned forward and smiled. "Miss Cassidy, I do believe you're asking me for another date."

She fluttered her eyelids and stared at the ceiling. "Why on earth would you think such a thought, Mr. Conrad?"

"Because," he said, "that's what I'm hoping you meant. Did you?"

Her mischievous attitude changed to a serious one. "Yes," she whispered.

He smiled. "Good. Then we'll do it again tomorrow night."

A frown line pulled at her forehead. "It will have to be later tomorrow night."

His eyebrows shot up. "Why? Do you have something else planned?"

She nodded. "I told Bill I'd come to work."

He released her hand and stared at her.

"What? You can't ride. Patches isn't ready, and I know enough about trick riding that the horse has to be really well trained with the rider they're carrying. You don't have another horse like that."

"I know. I'm not going to ride. I'll help the other performers backstage get ready for the show and do anything else I can to make the performance go smoothly."

He shook his head. "I don't like this, Cheyenne. The last time you were there, you were almost killed. We don't know who's trying to harm you, but it had to be somebody who got close enough to know your tack from the others. It's not safe for you there."

"It'll be okay, Luke. Bill and Trace will be there watching out for me."

The more she tried to defend her decision, the more upset he became. "I thought that's what I was doing. I guess that means that you don't need me around if you have them."

"I didn't say that. You're making too much of this. I'm tired of not working, and I need to do this."

He shook his head. "You don't need to do anything but stay safe. That's what I've been trying to do."

She looked around the restaurant before her gaze came back to him. "Oh, I see. So you're saying that our friendship hasn't been real. It's just you trying to keep me safe because that's what a police officer does."

"I didn't say that. What I meant is…"

"I know exactly what you meant," she huffed.

The anger on her face fueled his, too. He couldn't believe she was being so unreasonable. All he wanted to do was keep her safe, and she appeared to be saying that wasn't necessary. If that was the case, he'd back off and let her do as she pleased.

"I think it's time we left," he said, almost flinching at the icy tone of his voice.

She lifted her head, threw her napkin on the table and stood up. "That's fine with me. I'll go to the ladies' room, and you can settle up the bill." She pursed her lips. "Unless of course I misunderstood, and you want me to pay for my meal since you're only spending your time protecting me."

He pushed to his feet and glared at her. "Of course I don't expect you to pay. I'll take care of it and meet you by the hostess station."

She didn't say anything as she turned and flounced away. Jasmine had been emotional like that, too. It seemed she was always getting upset at something he'd said. Most of the time he didn't even know what it was. This was why he hadn't been involved with a woman in a long time. There was no understanding them, and you couldn't reason with them like you could a man. With a groan he pulled out his wallet, dumped some bills on the table and stormed toward the entrance.

By the time she joined him, he had settled down and was now feeling guilty for having upset her so. When she came out of the ladies' room, she looked contrite, too, but neither of them said anything as they walked to his car. Twenty minutes later they still hadn't spoken as they rode along the curving mountain road that led back to Little Pigeon Ranch.

He glanced at her from time to time, but she stared straight ahead without wavering. After a while he sighed and decided it was probably best that this had happened. Stop this relationship before it got a chance to get started. He had enough to worry about without guarding against everything he said or did in order to keep Cheyenne from being upset with him.

The thought had barely flashed in his mind when he spotted a vehicle bearing down on them at a high speed. He gritted his teeth. What kind of idiot would drive like that on a mountain road? Beside him Cheyenne straightened in her seat. She was staring at the side-view mirror with a look of disbelief on her face.

"That car is going way too fast," she said.

Luke nodded. "I know. I wonder if something is the matter."

Suddenly the vehicle swerved into the opposite lane and accelerated to pass them. Luke glanced out his window and realized it wasn't a car but a black truck that was crowding his lane. "Get over!" Luke yelled, as if the driver could hear him.

He glanced back at the truck and his heart dropped to the pit of his stomach. The window on the truck rolled down and Luke could see an arm clasping a gun extended from the person behind the wheel.

"Get down!" Luke yelled as he grabbed the back of Cheyenne's neck and forced her down.

He saw the flash and heard two bullets rip through his car, then they were crashing through the guardrail and picking up speed as they plunged down the mountain. He released Cheyenne and grabbed the steering wheel with both hands just as the air bags exploded. Then with a jarring impact, the car came to an abrupt halt against a tree.

For a moment he couldn't move, then he shook off the dazed feeling as he turned to stare at Cheyenne. With a strangled cry he pushed the air bag off her and touched her face. "Cheyenne, are you okay?" he said.

She didn't answer, and when he pulled his hand away, he felt a sticky substance on it. She was bleeding badly. He pushed his air bag away, twisted in the seat and put his arm around her as he gave her a little shake.

"Cheyenne, please wake up."

She didn't move, and the most hopeless feeling he'd ever had in his life ripped through him. She had to be all right. He had too much to tell her. She had to know he was sorry he had lost his temper at the restaurant, and he was sorry he wasn't able to keep her safe.

With a sinking heart, he realized that this was too much like the night of his father's accident, and Luke didn't think he could survive anything like that again.

He tightened his hold on her and gave her another slight shake. "Cheyenne, open your eyes." When she didn't move, he reached in his pocket and pulled out his cell phone.

"9-1-1," the voice on the other end said. "What is your emergency?"

"This is Deputy Luke Conrad. A truck forced my car off the road, and we're down the mountainside against a tree. We're on the road that goes to Little Pigeon Ranch."

"I have your location on GPS, Luke. Just sit tight. I'll get the rescue team out there. Are you hurt?"

"I think I'm okay, but Cheyenne Cassidy, who is with me, is unconscious. She needs help."

"They're leaving now and should be there in a few minutes."

Luke disconnected the call and turned back to Cheyenne. It was beginning to grow cold in the car. He reached for the ignition. If he could get the motor on, he could turn up the heater. He turned the key, but nothing happened. There had to be more damage to the car than he'd first thought.

Beside him Cheyenne groaned. She was wearing a jacket, but he felt her body shiver. He quickly pulled off his coat and wrapped it around her.

"Hang on, Cheyenne. There's help on the way."

TEN

Cheyenne awoke to bright lights shining in her face. She frowned and raised her arm to cover her eyes. Something about her surroundings seemed familiar, but she couldn't figure out what it was. She turned her head to the side and almost gasped when she saw Luke sitting in a chair beside her. He was bent forward with his hands covering his face and his elbows propped on his knees.

She tried to speak, but her throat was dry and his name came out of her mouth in a raspy sound. "Luke."

He immediately lowered his hands and sat up straight. A look of relief flooded his face as he stared down at her. "You're finally awake. The doctor said you'd come around when you were ready, but I was beginning to doubt he knew what he was talking about."

"Doctor?" she croaked. "Am I back in the hospital?"

"Yes. Do you remember what happened last night?"

She lay still for a moment and tried to recall what had happened after they left the restaurant. Slowly the thoughts began to form in her mind. "A truck. I remember a truck. He was going so fast, and then you grabbed my neck and pushed me down."

Luke nodded. "Someone shot at us. We went off the road and hit a tree. You've been unconscious ever since."

Cheyenne tried to push up in bed, but Luke put a restraining hand on her shoulder. "Don't sit up. You've had a bad bump on your head. The doctor ordered a CT scan, and it didn't show any internal injuries, which is why I couldn't figure out why you didn't wake up. You do have a bad cut across the back of your head. They put some staples in it, but you lost a lot of blood."

She frowned as she tried to take in all that he was saying. They'd been shot at and they'd gone down a mountainside? She closed her eyes and tried to remember, but she couldn't. It was rather frightening not to be able to recall something, but the fact that Luke was the first person she'd seen when she opened her eyes made it seem not as bad as it might have been. Her eyes closed for a moment as the guilt consumed her.

His hand squeezed her arm, and she heard his soft voice. "Cheyenne, are you all right? Do I need to call a nurse?"

She shook her head, opened her eyes and stared up at him. "I can't believe you stayed after the way I talked to you. I'm sorry, Luke. I didn't mean those things I said. Can you forgive me?" Her last word ended on a sob.

His face softened, and his hand gave another little squeeze on her arm. "I forgive you, but I was wrong, too. I overreacted to your going back to the Wild West show, and I shouldn't have. I don't have any right to tell you what to do. So I have to ask you to forgive me, too."

"Of course I do," she said. "You were only trying to help me." She was sure that she'd hurt him, a man who had been nothing but kind to her ever since they met. Suddenly the thought of losing his friendship was worse than what any stalker could do to her. She took a deep breath to dredge up the courage she needed to ask the question she had to. She feared the answer he might give. "So where do we go from here?"

His tired eyes raked her face, and a small smile curled his lips. "We've asked and given forgiveness. Now I think it's time to pick up where we left off and choose to forget what's happened."

Her heart beat in her chest so hard she thought she would burst. "I like that idea. The next time we get out of sorts with each other let's remember what it felt like when we were angry. I don't want to feel that way again."

"Neither do I," he whispered. "If anything had happened to you..."

She reached up and put her fingers on his lips. "But nothing did, and we're going to put this behind us."

He reached up, pulled her hand from his mouth and threaded their fingers together. "But there's one thing we can't overlook, and that's the guy who shot at us. He's getting bolder, Cheyenne. He attacked you last week, and last night he tried to kill both of us. We've got to find out who he is."

"Do you think we can?"

Luke sat back in his seat, rested his elbows on the chair arms and tented his fingers. As he tapped them together, he pursed his lips like he was deep in thought. Finally he inhaled and leaned forward. "I think so. I've been thinking about that all night. I don't think we can afford to wait around any longer for him to strike and hope we catch him. I think we're going to have to be aggressive and go after him."

"Aggressive?"

"I think your idea of going back to the Wild West show may be the answer, not because of your reason but because that's where he struck before. He was able to get close to you, close enough to cut your drag strap. It just stands to reason that he's walking among us, that he's somebody we all know and probably working there. A stranger would have stood out backstage, but someone who's there all the time would fit right in and have access to you."

Her heart thudded and she swallowed hard. "Are you asking me to go back and be a decoy?"

He nodded. "Yes."

"But last night you didn't want me anywhere near that place. You thought I'd be in danger."

"I still think you will be, but I'll be there with you. I know this is a lot to ask, but it may be our only chance of catching this guy. If you don't feel you're up to doing this, tell me. I won't force you to do anything you don't want to do."

She thought about it for a minute before she answered. "It may be the only way. So I'll do it."

A serious look came across his face and he scooted closer to the bed. "I want you to be sure about this, Cheyenne. You can't go back in there and act like you're scared. We can't do anything to tip him off. I'll talk to Bill and Trace and tell them what I want to do. They can help keep an eye out, too."

She took a deep breath. "Okay. When do we start?"

"As soon as the doctor dismisses you. He'll be by later to check on you. Jeff Swan has another guard posted outside your door. So I'm going to go home and take a shower, then I'll go over to Bill's place and talk to him. I'll come back by after that, and we'll see if the doctor's going to keep you longer or let you leave."

He started to push up from his chair, but Cheyenne reached out and grabbed his arm. "Wait. What about work? Aren't you supposed to be on the day shift today?"

He shook his head. "After I gave Ben my

statement about what happened last night, he gave me today off. So I'll come back here."

Although that's what she wanted, she also didn't want Luke to think she was monopolizing his time. "You don't have to do that," she said. "I know you have things you need to do, and I can't expect you to put your life on hold for me."

A smile creased his face as he leaned toward her. "We've only known each other a short time, Cheyenne, but you've already become very special to me. It's time this guy is stopped so you can get your life back, and I want to help you do that."

Her heart seemed to give a little flip at his words, and she struggled to hold back the tears. "Thank you, Luke. You've become special to me, too, and I appreciate everything you've done for me."

He smiled. "No need to thank me. Let's just concentrate on catching this guy."

"Okay," she murmured.

He stared at her for a moment longer, and her heart almost stopped. Then he took a step back and cleared his throat. "Get some rest, and I'll be back later."

With that he turned and walked to the door.

He was about to open it when she raised her head from the pillow and called out. "Luke, I really am sorry about our argument last night."

He turned around and frowned at her. Then he tilted his head to one side and bit down on his lip. After a moment he shook his head. "An argument? You must be mistaken. I don't remember anything about an argument."

Then he was gone out the door, and she let her head sink back to the bed. She pulled the covers up over her, smiled and then suddenly stilled as the truth washed over her. She'd once asked her mother how she would know when she was in love, and her mother had given the typical answer that she would just know.

At the time Cheyenne had thought that a ridiculous statement. Now she realized it was true. She was beginning to have thoughts about Luke Conrad that had to be ignored. She couldn't get on with her life until Jesse was caught. Until that time she needed to concentrate on what was important—catching the man who murdered her parents.

Luke found Bill and Trace Johnson in the main office at the Wild West show headquarters. Bill was seated at his desk, and Trace was peering over his dad's shoulder when Luke walked in. They both looked up in surprise when they saw him.

"Luke," Bill said. "Come in. Have you seen Cheyenne this morning?"

Luke nodded. "I have. She's awake and talking. The doctor is going to decide later if she can go home or not. But how did you know what happened?"

Trace straightened and walked around the desk. "Ben came by a while ago and told us. Dad and I had some last-minute details to take care of for tonight's performance, but I was planning on going to the hospital when I finished."

"I'm sure she'd like that. There's a guard outside her door. Just tell him who you are, and I'm sure he'll let you in."

Bill shook his head and leaned back in his chair. "I can't believe what she's been through in the last few years. This guy has upset her whole life. You know her dad was a friend of mine, and he coached Trace on his college rodeo team. To have him and his wife murdered and Cheyenne threatened is more than anybody ought to have to bear."

Luke nodded. "You're right. She needs help,

and that's why I'm here. I think together we may be able to catch this guy."

Trace walked around the desk and stopped beside Luke. "Just tell us what to do. Anything to help Cheyenne. You know we'll do it."

"That's what I was counting on," Luke said.

Quickly he laid out his plan to bring Cheyenne back to the show to work backstage with the goal of being able to get a lead on her stalker. When he'd finished, Bill nodded. "Do you really think Cheyenne's stalker might work for us?"

Luke shrugged. "I can't say for sure, but he has to be somebody with access to the backstage area. How else could he have cut her drag strap?"

"Then we'll do everything we can to help you," Trace said. "The sooner this guy is caught, the safer it will be for everybody around here. Who's not to say he might decide to go after one of our other employees?"

Luke nodded. "That's right. So I thought maybe she could come back tonight and work backstage. I'd like to tag along just to keep an eye on her and make sure everything goes okay. Is that a problem?"

Bill shook his head. "No problem. You've

been in the back enough times to know how things work. Just pitch in and give us a hand in getting the acts into the arena."

"I'll do it." Bill rose, and Luke leaned over the desk with his hand extended. "Thanks, Bill. Maybe we can catch this guy."

"I hope so," he said as they shook hands.

"And so do I," Trace added. "Anything you need me to do, let me know."

Luke glanced from one to the other. "Thanks, guys. I appreciate your help on this."

Bill waved his hand in dismissal. "No thanks needed. We're as eager to catch this pervert as you are, not only for Cheyenne's sake, but ours, too. I don't want word to get around that our show is a danger for its riders. That could be an incentive for the best riders to steer clear of us."

"Well, maybe we won't have to worry about that for long. I'll see you tonight," Luke said and headed for the door. As he stepped into the hallway, he spied a figure scurrying in the opposite direction, and his eyebrows arched.

Virgil Adkins seemed to be in a hurry, and Luke wondered why. Could he have been listening at the door while he was talking with Bill and Trace? He opened the door and stepped back into the office. Both men stared at him when he reentered.

"Did you forget something?" Bill asked.

"I forgot to ask something when I was here. How much do you know about Virgil Adkins? He's not from around here, and I wondered where he came from, what he's done in the past, things like that."

Trace's face had grown pale, and he swallowed hard before he spoke. "Why? Do you have reason to suspect he might be Cheyenne's stalker?"

"Nothing concrete. Just a feeling. I noticed the night of Cheyenne's accident he had a cut on his hand. He said it was from cutting the bindings on a hay bale, but it seemed coincidental. How long has he worked for you?"

Father and son glanced each other, and Bill gave a small shrug. "I'd say about six months. He was a drifter coming through town and needed a job. I needed somebody at the time to fill in because one of our employees who mucks out the stalls was on sick leave. He begged for a chance, and I let him do it. He proved to be good with horses. So I kept him on when my other worker came back." He turned to Trace. "Did you do that background check on him like I asked you to?"

Trace bit down on his lip, and he nodded. "I did."

Bill rose from his chair, leaned his fists on the desk and glared at Trace. "I don't like the way you said that. Did you find out something I need to know."

Trace glanced from Luke to his father and licked his lips. "Dad, the guy was down and out. He needed a helping hand, and he begged me to give him a chance."

"Another chance because of what?" Bill roared as his eyebrows shot to his hairline.

Trace's face had grown paler at his father's loud voice, and he dropped his head and stared at the floor. "He'd been arrested several times for theft. Never anything much, just petty stuff, but he was found guilty. He had to make restitution and serve community service hours."

"A thief?" Bill thundered. "You let me hire a known thief? Son, your good intentions are going to get you in trouble one of these days. And this may be one of those times."

Trace shook his head. "I don't think so. He's done a good job for us."

"But we don't know what he's doing when

he's not here," Bill said and then turned back to Luke. "What do you want to do now?"

Luke shook his head. "Nothing. I'll keep an eye on him. If he's up to something, I'll catch him."

Bill directed another glare at his son and then turned back to Luke. "We'll be watching, too. Won't we, Trace?"

Trace nodded. "I'm sorry, Dad. I won't do anything like that again."

Bill leaned toward him. "You'd better not if you know what's good for you."

Luke swallowed back the shock he felt. He had never heard Bill talk like that to Trace before, and he wondered if it was normal. From the look on Trace's face it was something he'd experienced quite often. Luke narrowed his eyes and studied Bill's angry face. The relationship between father and son was really none of his business.

He cleared his throat, and they both turned to face him. "I'll go and let you two get back to work, but I'll be here with Cheyenne tonight. In the meantime, if you think of anything that might help us catch this guy, give me a call." He turned and hurried out of the office. When he closed the door behind him, he heard a raised voice inside. He couldn't tell what was being said, but he knew it was Bill Johnson doing all the talking. His voice seemed to grow louder with each word.

It was time for him to get out of here. The Johnsons could work out their own problems. He had the murder attempts on his and Cheyenne's lives to worry about, and that was all he needed to think about now.

ELEVEN

Cheyenne walked down the alleyway in the backstage area of the Wild West show as she led Kerry Hilliard's mare, Sparkles, toward a stall at the back. At the moment Kerry was in the arena performing as one of the passengers in a stagecoach that was being chased by outlaws. She could hear the crowd cheering as the fake gunshots echoed through the building, and she smiled.

She was glad to be back at the show. In the week since Patches's injury she had missed riding and being around people who shared her interests. When the doctor had told her earlier today that she wasn't going to have to stay in the hospital, she'd been thrilled that she and Luke had the chance to put his plan into action. She'd hoped that whoever was behind the threats would be discovered right away, but that hadn't been the case.

So far nothing had happened. Truthfully, though, she'd been so busy she hardly had time to think about it. From the moment she'd arrived, she'd been busy with the riders' horses, just like she was now. That suited her fine. The performers wanted their horses to be groomed to perfection when they entered the ring, and she was happy to oblige them tonight.

She loved working with horses and caring for them. In fact it was all she'd ever known. Living on a horse-breeding ranch had taught her a lot about working with these magnificent animals, and she enjoyed every minute she spent with one. She just hoped it wouldn't be too long before Patches was back to normal, and they could start training again. As it stood now, however, her return to performing looked like it was months away.

She sighed in resignation as she reached the stall where she'd been grooming other horses tonight and led Sparkles inside. The horse stopped and eyed the stall with doubt and gave a whinny as she shifted her feet. "Come on, girl," Cheyenne murmured as she gave a tug on the lead.

Sparkles tossed her head and followed Cheyenne into the stall. Still talking quietly to the horse, Cheyenne tied the lead in a highwayman's hitch quick-release knot to a rail on the side of the stall. You never could tell when a horse might spook and pull on the rope. She'd heard of horses' necks being broken because of such an incident, and she didn't want to experience anything like that.

Once she had Sparkles settled, she ran her hand down the horse's leg and gently squeezed the tendon. Sparkles cooperated by picking up her foot. Using a hoof pick, Cheyenne began to remove the debris that had gathered underneath.

She was concentrating on her task so much that she didn't hear Luke stop at the opening of the stall. "Need any help?" he asked in a soft voice.

Cheyenne looked up at him and smiled. "No, thanks. I've got this. Where have you been?"

"Just trying to help out back here and blend in as well as I can. I hope you didn't think I'd deserted you. I was keeping an eye on you all the time and knew what you were doing."

She laughed and shook her head. "I'm fine. I'll be sure to yell if anything happens, though."

"You do that. In the meantime, I'm enjoying seeing the show from the other side of the curtain, so to speak. Someone who hasn't gotten to witness what goes on behind the scenes wouldn't believe the amount of work and the precision it takes to pull off a perfect performance."

She nodded and went back to her task. "I know. It has to be like a well-oiled machine back here." He didn't say anything for a moment, and she looked up. His eyes were fixed on her, and a small smile curled his lips. "What?" she asked.

He just shook his head. "Nothing. I was just thinking how natural you look grooming that horse."

"I should," she answered. "My father taught me well. He expected our animals to be well-cared for, and he demanded I take my job seriously."

"I think I would have liked your dad," Luke said, his voice soft.

Tears filled her eyes, and she raised her head to stare at him. "I think you would have, too. And I know he would have liked you."

She saw the muscles in Luke's throat ripple as he swallowed, and then he glanced over his shoulder. "I hear the music getting louder. That means the performers will be riding out of the arena any minute. I'd better go see if I can help." He started to turn away. "Are you okay with me leaving you alone?"

"Sure, go on."

"I won't be gone long."

She nodded and didn't look up as she heard him walk away. Thirty minutes later she was just finishing up when she heard footsteps again and glanced up to see Trace Johnson entering the stall. He stopped and let his gaze drift over Sparkles. "She looks good, Cheyenne. Thanks for helping out tonight. Kerry is so busy, I know she appreciates you taking care of her horse for her."

Cheyenne glanced up and sucked in her breath at the sad look on Trace's face. She'd seen that look before when he'd been on her dad's rodeo team, and she knew what it meant. He and his father had argued again. Or should she say, Bill had argued. Trace never had learned to stand up to his dad.

"Are you okay, Trace?" she asked.

He bit down on his lip and gave a slight nod. "Yeah. It's just been one of those days. You know how Dad gets when he's worried about something. It's easy for him to vent on me. I should be used to it by now, but every time it happens, I feel worse than I did the last time."

She checked Sparkles to make sure she was tied securely, then walked over to Trace. She put her hand on his arm and looked into his eyes. "Trace, he loves you. He just reacts sometimes before he thinks."

Trace sighed. "Yeah, and it's getting worse as time goes by." He stared at her, and the sad look in his eyes pierced her heart. "I don't know what to do, Cheyenne. I want to leave, but he needs me to help with the business. So I'm stuck. I can't decide what to do."

"You need to do whatever makes you happy, Trace."

He exhaled and raked his hand through his hair. "You're right, and the only one who can make that decision is me."

"That's right, and I know you'll make the right one."

He nodded and looked past her to the horse. "Well, I'm not going to decide tonight. So in the meanwhile, have you finished here so we can get Kerry's horse back to her regular stall?"

Cheyenne looked back at the horse. "I'm

almost through. I need some of that super-shine hoof polish for her. I looked in the cabinet where it's kept before I came in here, but I didn't see any."

Trace closed his eyes for a moment and groaned. "Oh, no. I was supposed to pick up some this afternoon, but I forgot. I hope no one has said anything to Dad about our being out. He'll have my head for not getting it."

Cheyenne could see the tenseness in Trace's body, and she put her hand on his shoulder. "Don't worry about it. You can get some tomorrow."

He shook his head. "No, I'd better do it tonight. Dad keeps some petty cash in his desk for small purchases. I'll get some of it and run over to Wrangler Supply before he notices. I'll check with you when I get back."

He turned, rushed out of the stall and collided with Luke, who was about to enter. "Sorry, Luke," he mumbled as he hurried away.

Luke stepped inside and looked back at Trace running down the alleyway. "What's he in such a hurry for?"

"He forgot to buy hoof polish, and he's trying to get some before his dad finds out."

Luke arched his eyebrows. "I can under-

stand why. I was a witness at his father's ti-
rade today. I felt sorry for Trace."

She nodded. "Yeah. It's been that way ever
since I've known them. When Trace was on
my dad's rodeo team, Bill used to come to
every rodeo Trace was in. It seemed like he
could never please his father. He would yell
at him in front of the other guys and tell him
how disappointed he was in him. Even when
he had a great ride, it wasn't good enough. He
always had to do better."

Luke glanced back once more in the direction that Trace had gone. "I've known them
for several years now, and I never suspected
something like that. It just goes to show you
that you never know what's going on in someone else's life."

"That's right. I just wish…"

She never got to finish her statement because Kerry walked in at that moment. A
smile flashed across her face as she caught
sight of her horse. "Oh, Cheyenne," she murmured as she stepped closer. "She looks so
good. Thank you for doing this for me. This
is really a busy night, and now we have to ride
in the relay race."

"I was glad to do it, Kerry. I hope your team wins."

She chuckled as she patted Sparkles and then released the slip knot. "We're going to try our best, aren't we, girl?" she said as she led the horse toward the opening in the stall. "I'll see you later."

"Later," Cheyenne answered.

Luke stepped closer and began to help her pack up her grooming kit. When the last brush and comb were inside, he glanced at her. "You ready to go back up to the front. There's a spot there with a view of the arena. We can watch the riders perform?"

She nodded. "I'd like that."

Before they could take a step to leave, Trace suddenly reappeared in the door, his eyes wild. "Luke, I'm glad you're still here. I need you to come with me."

"What's wrong?" Luke asked.

"Somebody's been in our office," he said as he turned and ran down the alleyway with Luke right behind him.

Cheyenne closed her grooming kit and set it against the side of the stall before she took out after the two men. By the time she reached the office, they were both behind Bill's desk.

"I came to get some money out of the petty cash to go make a purchase, and this is what I found. The drawer looks like it's been rifled through, and the money is gone."

"Somebody took the money?" Cheyenne asked as she inched forward.

Luke frowned and shook his head. "We don't know that for sure. Maybe Bill put the money somewhere else."

"I put what money somewhere else?" a voice asked.

They all looked around to see Bill Johnson standing at the door. Trace stepped from the back of the desk. "I came in to get some money out of the petty cash, and there wasn't any in the box."

Bill frowned and walked over to the desk. "What do you mean there isn't any money it the box? I checked this afternoon, and there was three hundred dollars inside."

"Well, there's none in it now," Luke said.

Bill's mouth dropped open, and he looked from Luke to Trace. "What could have happened to it?"

"Maybe somebody took it, Dad," Trace said.

Bill stared back down at the desk for a moment, and then he nodded. "Well, it was no secret that I kept a small amount of cash, but I trusted everybody who works here." He paused a moment and glared at Trace. "That is until this morning when I found out I had a thief on my payroll."

Cheyenne sucked in her breath at the angry look on Bill's face and glanced at Luke. He shook his head. "Now, Bill, we can't make any accusations until we have some evidence."

Bill nodded. "You're right. Maybe I have something that will spread some light on the matter."

"What's that?"

Bill smiled. "I had an irate customer come in a few months ago demanding his money back. It seemed he didn't like the show. When I wouldn't give him a refund, he became very angry. One of the wranglers heard it and came in. Then the man threatened him. For a few minutes there I thought I was going to have to call Ben, but the angry customer left after he was through ranting. I installed surveillance cameras all over the place after that. You never know what somebody like that will do." He pointed toward a bookshelf across the room. "There's one over there."

They all turned to look in the direction Bill was pointing. "Where?" Luke asked.

"The black box sitting beside the books on the shelf."

Cheyenne squinted and looked closer at the rectangular box that blended in with its surroundings. She glanced at Luke, and he had his gaze fixed on it, too. "Can we review the footage?"

Bill nodded. "Sure. It's hooked to my computer. Let's check it out."

Bill sat down and turned on his computer. Trace and Luke stood behind him. Cheyenne waited a moment, but when no one suggested she join them, she took a deep breath and edged around beside Luke until she had a good view of the computer screen.

Bill quickly forwarded through the footage for a few minutes until he suddenly stopped and allowed the recording to play. No one moved or said a word as a figure approached the desk. His head was bent as he moved behind the desk and carefully pulled the drawer open. Then he rifled inside and pulled out a wad of bills that he stuffed in his pocket before he closed the drawer. He stepped back from the desk, and for the first time raised his head so that his full face was in view.

Cheyenne's mouth gaped open, and she covered it with her hand as she recognized the man in the recording. "Virgil Adkins," she gasped.

She glanced around at Luke. The muscle in his jaw was twitching, and he had an angry look on his face. His eyes narrowed as they fastened on her. "Yes, Virgil Adkins," he muttered. "The man who had a cut on his hand the night your tack was sabotaged." He turned his attention to Bill. "We need to find Virgil right now. He has some explaining to do."

Virgil Adkins sat in a chair in Bill Johnson's office and glared at Luke and Ben Whitman. "Why did you bring me in here? Just because you fired me tonight don't mean I done something wrong."

"Really?" Luke asked. "Maybe you're forgetting what happened earlier when you came into this room."

Virgil shook his head. "I didn't come in here tonight. I've been helping get the horses ready all night."

Luke shook his head. "I talked with some of

your coworkers before you came in. They said you'd worked with them most of the night, but you had taken a break for about fifteen minutes. They had no idea where you'd gone."

"I went outside to take a smoke. We can't smoke in the barn area because it's a fire hazard."

Ben, who'd been silent, stood up and stared down at Virgil. "Did you happen to take a detour on your way back and stop by Bill's office?"

"I told you I ain't been in here tonight," Virgil muttered. "And you can't prove I did."

"Oh, we think we can. You may have known there was petty cash in Bill's drawer, but you didn't know there was a surveillance camera in the room. We have the footage of you taking the money, so you might as well own up to it."

Virgil's face grew red, and he shook his head. "I don't care what you think you have, it wasn't me. If you don't believe me, search me and see if you find any money on me."

Before they could respond, he jumped to his feet and emptied his pockets onto Bill's desk. When he'd finished, he pulled the lining out to show there was nothing left inside. He looked up at them with a smug smile. "See. Nothing."

Ben and Luke glanced at each other, and Ben grinned. "Don't play games with me, Adkins. I've been a lawman a long time. You're a petty crook who's stolen before, and you took three hundred dollars tonight from Bill's desk. It's in your best interest to cooperate with us before it gets worse."

Virgil folded his arms across his chest. "I ain't saying nothing."

Ben shrugged. "Have it your way."

A knock sounded at the door, and Luke went to open it. Another deputy from their office stood in the hallway with an envelope in his hand. He looked past Luke to Ben as he handed the envelope to Luke. "Here's what you asked for, Ben. Do you need any more help?"

Ben shook his head. "No, Murphy. You can continue with your patrol. Luke and I have this."

The deputy touched the brim of his hat and tipped it before he turned and left. Luke walked back to Ben and gave him the envelope. Virgil stared as Ben opened it and pulled out a sheet of paper.

"What's that?"

Ben cocked an eyebrow at Virgil and shook his head. "Just a court order. A judge signed saying that we can search your apartment, your locker and anything else of your personal property. Any chance you want to change your story now?"

Virgil blinked, and for a moment Luke thought he detected a look of fear in his eyes. Then he took a deep breath. "No. I'm not changing anything."

"Have it your way," Ben said as he and Luke each took him by the arm and guided him out of the room.

Bill and Trace stood outside in the hall, along with Cheyenne. Ben nodded to Bill. "Do you have the combination to Virgil's locker?"

"I do."

"Then let's go open it." Bill led the way down the hallway and into a room that was lined with lockers. Bill walked to one on the far side and stopped in front of it. "We give each of our employees a locker to keep their coats and personal articles in."

Luke frowned. "Did Cheyenne not have one? I remember the night she performed I had to get her coat from your office."

"That was an oversight. I'd meant to assign her one, but somehow it didn't get done. I told her to leave her things in my office that night, and we'd get her one the next day."

Luke inclined his head toward the one in front of Bill. "But this is Virgil's locker?"

"Yes."

"Then let's open it."

Virgil fidgeted beside Luke as Bill began to dial the combination. After a few seconds it clicked, and Bill pulled the door open. Luke stepped forward and stared inside. There was nothing inside that he could see except for Virgil's jacket, which was folded and lay on a shelf at the top.

As he pulled out the jacket, it suddenly unfolded in his hands and he heard a thump at his feet. He stared down at the small canvas bag that had hit the floor. Virgil stiffened and tried to take a step back, but Ben held on to him.

Luke picked up the bag, unzipped it and gave a soft whistle at what he saw inside. He glanced at Ben and then at Virgil as he pulled out a wad of bills and held them up. "How much money do you think this could be? Maybe three hundred dollars?"

Virgil clamped his mouth shut and glared at Luke.

"Put your hands behind your back," Ben ordered. "You're under arrest for theft. It'll be up to Mr. Johnson whether or not he wants to press charges, but with your record a judge might not look too favorably on this."

"Wait a minute," Luke said. "There's more."

Ben snapped the handcuffs in place on Virgil and looked up. "What?"

"This," Luke said as he pulled the other item he'd seen inside the bag, a music box that looked very similar to the one he'd seen in the video that Cheyenne received.

He walked to the door and opened it. She still stood outside with Trace. "Cheyenne, could you come here a minute?"

She cast a quizzical glance in his direction and nodded before she followed him into the room. "What is it?"

Luke held out the music box. "Can you identify this?"

Her gaze dropped to his hand, and her face went pale. Her body began to tremble "That's my music box," she said, "the one that was stolen from my room when it was ransacked."

Virgil took a step toward Luke, but Ben grabbed him by the arm. "I ain't never seen that box in my life," he yelled.

"Then what's it doing in your locker with the money you stole from Bill's office?" Luke asked.

The veins in Virgil's neck were standing out, and he tried once again to move toward Luke. "That's close enough," Ben growled, but Virgil continued to glare at Luke.

Luke turned back to Ben and arched his eyebrows. Ben gave a slight nod, tightened his hold on Virgil and guided him toward the door. "Virgil Adkins," he said, "you are under arrest for stalking, theft and for the attempted murders of Cheyenne Cassidy and Luke Conrad. You have the right to an attorney and the right to remain silent. Anything you say may be used in a court of law. Do you understand your rights?"

Virgil just grunted and cast one last angry glance toward Luke and Cheyenne before Ben forced him into the hall. "I ain't sayin' another word until I get a lawyer."

Luke watched them go for a moment before he looked back at Cheyenne. She looked as if she was in shock. Her eyes were wide, and her body was rigid. She was so still he wondered if she was even breathing.

He took a step toward her. "Cheyenne?"

Tears began to roll down her cheeks. "Is it over? Is it really over at last?"

Behind her Trace Johnson walked into the room. He reached out and touched her arm. "Cheyenne, you're safe now."

It didn't appear like she heard him or was even aware of his presence. All she could do was stare at Luke. Then with a cry she pushed off on one foot and launched herself at him. He caught her and wrapped his arms around her as she buried her face in his neck.

Her warm tears ran onto his skin, and he tightened his arms around her as her body shook with sobs. He closed his eyes and kissed the top of her head. "Don't cry," he whispered. "Everything's going to be all right now. I promise you."

Her only answer was to snuggle closer to him, and in that moment he realized how much she had come to mean to him. He'd known that God must have a woman for him, but after Jasmine he'd begun to give up hope. Then Cheyenne had run out in front of his car, and he knew that had to be the best day of his life.

God had sent him the one he needed, a woman who was nothing like his ex. A woman he'd come to love.

TWELVE

Cheyenne couldn't believe how peaceful it had been for the past week since Virgil Adkins had been arrested. The texts, emails and calls had stopped, indicating that he was indeed her stalker.

But she was hesitant to accept that her ordeal was over. If Virgil Adkins hadn't stolen that money, they wouldn't have caught him. She just couldn't believe that someone who'd tormented her for so long would be so careless.

They also hadn't been able to link his computer or his cell phone to her. Luke told her to be patient, that solving a case was just a matter of following the trail the perpetrator left, and the police felt sure Virgil had slipped up somewhere. She just appreciated their dedication to the task. And with each passing day her hope that her torture had truly come to an end increased.

"Penny for your thoughts." Gwen's voice shattered her preoccupation.

Cheyenne gave a startled gasp as she looked down at the spatula she held. Minutes ago she had been icing the cake that would be served at Christmas dinner tomorrow. Now the gooey frosting was dripping on the table.

She laid down the spatula and grabbed a kitchen towel as she began to mop up the mess. "I'm so sorry, Gwen. I let my mind wander for a few minutes."

Her friend just chuckled. "I thought for a moment you might be going to sleep. Then I wondered if you were thinking about a certain someone we all know."

Cheyenne shook her head, and glanced back down at the cake. "No, I was trying to convince myself that my ordeal is over and that Virgil Adkins will be punished for what he did to me."

A small frown puckered Gwen's forehead as she dried her hands on her apron. "Cheyenne, I know it's been difficult, but you're safe now. Tomorrow is Christmas, and we're going to have a wonderful day."

Tears pooled in her eyes as she thought of how different it was going to be this year. "I'm so glad I'm here and so thankful you and Dean want me to share the holiday with you. I don't know what I'd do if you hadn't come into my life."

Gwen walked over, put her arm around Cheyenne's waist and gave her a hug. "We're thankful you're here. Ever since you walked through the door to rent a room from us, I knew that we were going to have a special bond. Now you're family, and you always will be."

Cheyenne bit down on her lip and blinked back her tears. "It's so good to have family again. Especially at Christmas." She rubbed the palm of her hand across her eyes, sniffed and then straightened her back. "I'm looking forward to spending tomorrow with all of you, but I'm really excited about seeing Maggie open her presents in the morning."

Gwen's eyebrows shot up. "Well, it may take a while for her to do that. I haven't been able to stop Dean from buying 'just one more thing,' as he kept saying. Now there's a stack of gifts as high as a mountain." She stopped speaking, and a wistful expression covered her face. "Of course I don't mind. He wants to make up for all the Christmases he missed with her."

Cheyenne didn't say anything, just nodded. She knew Dean and Gwen's story and how they had divorced without Gwen telling Dean she was expecting a baby. He hadn't known about Maggie's existence until she was about five years old, but now they were reunited in the home Dean had inherited from his grandfather. It was the most welcoming place Cheyenne had ever experienced. Dean and Gwen deserved this, and she was so glad they were letting her be a part of it.

"So," Gwen continued as she turned back to the sink and the dishes stacked there, "is Luke going to be able to join us for dinner tomorrow?"

Cheyenne directed her attention back to the cake and didn't look at Gwen as she answered. "Yes. Ben has scheduled him for an early morning shift, so he should be off in time for dinner."

Gwen loaded several pans into the dishwasher before she straightened and put her hands on her hips. "You've been seeing a lot of Luke for the past few weeks. I can tell he likes you."

Cheyenne concentrated on the cake in front of her. "I don't know," she murmured. "I'm sure he's just being nice."

Cheyenne looked up when Gwen didn't say anything. She was standing with her arms crossed and her eyebrows arched. "Nice, huh? Cheyenne, the man more than *likes* you. I can tell."

Her heartbeat quickened, but she didn't know what to say. She knew Luke liked her, and she liked him. She just didn't know if it was enough or not. After all, she hadn't been honest with him, and she'd been the reason his life had been in danger. It was better not to wish for something that might never come to be.

Cheyenne shook her head and swiped the spatula across the top of the cake. "You're just imagining things."

"I'm not. Why are you reluctant to believe it?"

She quit what she was doing and stared at Gwen. "I told him my whole story. He knows how I met my stalker in a chat room and how I kept that information from the police. I'm not proud of that. In fact I'm very ashamed and feel guilty about my parents' deaths. I don't think I'm the kind of person he would ever trust, and especially not one he would want a relationship with."

Gwen shook her head. "You're wrong about that. I think you're being too hard on yourself."

Cheyenne shook her head. "No, I've thought about this a lot since Virgil was caught, and I think if Luke has any interest in me, it will start to wane now that I'm out of trouble. I've tried to get past my guilt, but I can't. I've asked God to forgive me, and I feel that He has. The problem is that I can't forgive myself."

A sad look entered Gwen's eyes, and she took a step toward Cheyenne. "You have to quit thinking like that."

Cheyenne put the last of the icing on the cake and put the spatula back in the bowl. Then she jerked off the apron she was wearing and placed the bowl in the sink. She grasped the edge of the sink with both hands for a moment and stood with her head bowed and her eyes closed. Then she took a deep breath and turned toward the door. "I can't talk about this anymore. I'm going to the barn. I'll be back later."

Before Gwen could respond, Cheyenne bolted out the back door and headed down to the barn. What she needed was to spend time with Patches. That always calmed her down so she could think straight. And one thing she needed to put in perspective was Luke Conrad. He'd been kind to her, and she had feelings for him.

Although the thought pierced her heart, she knew what she should do. She needed to start easing away from their relationship so he could find someone who was much more suitable for him than she was. However, tomorrow was Christmas, and she wanted him to be at Dean and Gwen's house with her. After Christmas would be the best time.

Shaking thoughts of Luke from her head, she entered the stall where Patches had been resting since the night of their fall. The horse was always glad to see her, and he let out a loud whinny when he caught sight of her. She stopped beside him and began to stroke his neck as she spoke softly to him. How she'd missed riding him, but if he kept progressing like he was, they should be able to resume training maybe in the early spring.

"Ready for some cold compresses, boy?" she whispered in his ear, and she smiled when his tail swished. "Good. We'll get this over with, then I'll take you outside for a walk."

Thirty minutes later she led Patches from the barn into the corral next to it. This had been a routine since the fall, and Patches seemed to know what was expected. He followed along docilely as they entered the corral and began to circle the area.

They were on their third lap when she heard a truck drive up and stop. A grin pulled at her mouth when Luke climbed out and walked toward the corral. She led Patches over to the side and waited for him to join them. He stopped just on the other side of the wooden slats that made up the sides of the corral and grinned.

"How do you like my new truck?" he asked.

Cheyenne studied the shiny black vehicle for a moment before she smiled and nodded. "I like it a lot. When did you get it?"

He pushed the cowboy hat he wore back on his head and looked over his shoulder at it again. "This morning. My car was totaled, so this time I decided to go back to a truck. What do you think?"

"I really like it, and it looks like it would be good for hauling stuff. Are you planning on using it for that?"

He shrugged. "Maybe," he said.

When he didn't say anything else, Cheyenne spoke. "Did you come out for something other than to show me your new truck?"

He took a deep breath and nodded. "Yeah. I'd like to talk to you. Do you think you could put Patches in the barn and go to the house with me?"

The tone of his voice and the look on his face made her heart drop to the pit of her stomach. He sounded as if he needed to tell her something important, and she could only guess what it was. He'd come to let her know that since her stalker had been caught, it was time for them to move on with their lives.

She could just imagine how the conversation would go. He would explain that he had enjoyed getting to know her and that he would always be her friend, but they needed to explore other options. The meaning would be clear. He wanted to find someone else more suitable for him. Someone he could trust.

She should feel relieved. After all that's what she'd felt was going to happen. Somehow, though, now all it did was make her sad. She didn't want to end whatever was between them.

But she'd faced worse in her life so she put

on a brave face, forced a smile and nodded. "I'll be right back."

When her horse was safely back in his stall, she walked outside, where Luke was still waiting for her. He fell into step beside her as they headed back to the house, but neither one of them spoke. As they entered the house, she led him to the den, where they'd enjoyed decorating the Christmas tree together. The lights burned on it, and Cheyenne remembered what a good time they'd had.

She'd almost reached the sofa when she realized Luke wasn't behind her. He had stopped and was closing the door. Then he turned around and walked slowly to where she stood. A small smile pulled at his lips. "I love Maggie, but I wanted some private time without her interrupting us."

Cheyenne felt as if her heart had stopped, but she tried not to let it show. "You never can tell where Maggie is these days. She's taken to eavesdropping on all of us to try and find out Christmas secrets. I even found her hidden in the hall closet the other day."

"Maggie is very special to me, but I don't need her as an audience for what I have to say."

The serious look on his face and his words

made Cheyenne's knees tremble, and she sank to the couch. Earlier she'd thought she was prepared to see the end of their relationship, but now that she knew he was about to do it, she wished with all her heart it didn't have to be.

He walked slowly to her and sat down on the couch beside her. He reached over and took her hand in his and stared down at their laced fingers for a moment before he spoke. "Cheyenne," he murmured, "I have something to tell you."

Her heart thudded, and she thought she was going to burst into tears. "All right, Luke."

He hesitated a moment. "I don't really know how to say this."

She could see he was struggling, and she didn't want to prolong the agony. She squeezed his hand and leaned closer to him. "The best way is just to treat it like a Band-Aid."

"A Band-Aid?" He stared at her with a puzzled look on his face.

She nodded. "Yes. When you have something to say that's difficult to say to the other person, you just blurt it out, rip it off like a Band-Aid. It might hurt for a moment, but the pain will be gone soon."

He furrowed his eyebrows and tilted his

head to one side. "But I don't want to blurt it out. I've been trying for days to think of the best way to say this."

She sighed and pulled her hand away. "Luke, just say it. I can handle it."

He took a deep breath. "A few years ago I was hurt badly by a woman who I thought cared about me. She didn't. When I found out how she had deceived me, I was devastated. Then I was angry. Ever since, I've told myself I would never take a chance on being hurt like that again."

"I can understand that," Cheyenne said in a soft voice.

"All my friends have tried to set me up with someone since then, but I've never been interested, until now."

"U-until n-now?"

Luke nodded. "I know we only met a few weeks ago, but we've been through more in that time than a lot of people experience in a lifetime. It didn't take me long to know you were one of a kind, and that I wanted to know you more. I've enjoyed every minute we've spent together."

Her heart pounded in her chest. There it was. He'd enjoyed their time together, but now it was over. "Luke, it's all right. I understand. There's nothing for you to feel badly about."

A surprised look flashed across his face. "Feel badly? What do I have to feel badly about? I'm happier than I've ever been in my life, and it's all because of you." He leaned forward and cupped her chin in his hand. "Cheyenne Cassidy, I think we might have something good here, and I'd like to explore it. What do you say? Would you like to see where it leads?"

Luke felt her body jerk, and then she sat up straight. The wild look in her eyes made him frown, but it was her words that surprised him most. "What? I can't believe it."

He shook his head. "Why not? I thought you knew what I was trying to tell you."

She jumped to her feet and stared down at him. "I thought you were getting ready to tell me you didn't want to see me anymore, that our relationship was over."

He rose to his feet and moved just inches from her. "Why would you think that?"

"Because you're an officer of the law. I thought you were being nice to me because of that. I wasn't honest with you, and I was the reason you were almost killed. That doesn't make for a very good relationship."

He frowned and leaned closer to her. "That doesn't make any difference to me. I thought you could see the signs that I really liked you."

She threw up her hands in frustration. "What signs? You've never given me any signs about how you feel."

He gritted his teeth and took another step toward her. "Then maybe you'll understand this one."

Before she could answer, he wrapped his arms around her, pulled her to him and pressed his lips against hers. Her body went rigid for a moment, and then it was as if she melted against him as she returned his kiss.

He'd never felt such happiness flowing through him. He didn't want to release her, but he pulled away a few inches and stared down into her eyes, which held a dreamy look. "How's that for a sign?"

A slow smile pulled at her lips. "The best one you could give me."

"Did you really think I wanted to end it with you?"

She gave a slight nod. "Yes. I thought after I told you all about how I met Jesse, you wouldn't want to have anything to do with me anymore."

"I thought we had this settled," he growled. "That we weren't going to remember those things again."

"Maybe I'll be able to do that if I have you there to help me."

His heart gave a little lurch, and he smiled. "Does that mean what I hope it means?"

She reached up and stroked his cheek with her fingers. "I want to see where this goes, Luke, and I'm so thankful you came into my life."

"Tomorrow's going to be the best Christmas I've ever had," Luke whispered as he pulled her closer.

"For me, too," she whispered. "I'm so glad Ben gave you a shift that allowed you to come here for dinner."

"I'm off tonight, too. How about if I come back and spend Christmas Eve with you?"

"I'll look forward to it. Can you come for dinner? Gwen wants to eat at about six o'clock because she has so much to do for Christmas tomorrow."

He nodded. "I'll be here. Maybe we can go

into town and see all the Christmas lights afterward if you don't need to help Gwen."

"That sounds like fun. I think she wants to do some cooking for tomorrow and has some gifts to wrap. She said it was a one-woman job."

He glanced down at his watch. "I have to go. Our department has collected gifts for children in the hospital, and I'm helping Ben pass them out this afternoon."

She directed a teasing grin at him. "Are you going to dress up like Santa Claus?"

He couldn't help but laugh as he reached over and tapped the tip of her nose with his finger. "No, I'm not. I'm the elf."

Her eyes grew wide, and then she burst out laughing. "An elf? Are you wearing an elf costume?"

He huffed out a breath as if he was offended. "I am, and I have to say it looks good on me."

She continued to smile as she stared at him, then she suddenly threw her arms around his neck and pulled his head down until their lips almost touched. "You're one of a kind, Luke Conrad"

She pressed her lips to his, and he felt as if he was soaring on a cloud. When he pulled back from her, he whispered against her lips. "If you like the idea of me as an elf so much, I just may wear it to dinner tomorrow."

She giggled. "Maggie would love it."

He planted a soft kiss on her lips and released his hold on her. "I really have to go. I'll see you later."

She slipped her arm through his and smiled. "I'll see you to the door."

Together they strolled into the hallway and were almost to the door when a knock sounded on the outside. Cheyenne released Luke's arm and opened the door to see Trace Johnson standing on the front porch.

"Trace," she said, "how good to see you. Come on in."

He frowned as he glanced at Luke. "I hope I'm not disturbing you, but I wanted to come check on you."

Luke shook his head and stepped onto the porch. "I was just leaving. I have some Christmas errands to run." He stuck out his hand to Trace. "I hope you and your dad have a good Christmas."

Trace smiled as he shook Luke's hand. "Thanks, Luke. I think this is going to be the best Christmas I've ever had. I've got big plans."

For some reason the tone of Trace's words made a chill run down his back. He let his gaze drift over him, but he didn't seem any different than usual. Perhaps he'd read something in to the statement that was wrong. "That's good," Luke said as he glanced back at Cheyenne. "I'll see you later."

She lifted her hand and waved to him. "Later."

Luke hopped down the steps and started toward his truck, but he stopped and turned back to stare at the house. Cheyenne was holding the door open for Trace to enter. He smiled down at her before he stepped through the door, and then it closed.

Trace's words echoed in his mind once more. His voice had had almost a sinister sound to it. *Big plans.* What did he mean by that?

Luke glanced at the house once more and then shook his head. Trace was Cheyenne's friend. There was nothing to be concerned about.

Right?

THIRTEEN

"This is a nice surprise," Cheyenne said to Trace as she closed the front door. "I'm glad you came by to wish me a merry Christmas. I had intended to get over to your dad's house to see both of you, but I've been busy helping Gwen get ready for tomorrow. She and Dean want to make this a special Christmas for Maggie."

"Christmas is always exciting when there's a child to share it with," he said.

She chuckled. "Yes, it is, and Maggie can hardly wait for it. I think she's picked up every gift under the tree and shaken it, but I want her to enjoy it. I remember how special it was for me as a child. So what are you and your dad doing tomorrow?"

"Not much. Dad always buys a Christmas dinner from Joanne's diner, and we'll eat that.

Maybe watch some TV. I thought I might come by tomorrow afternoon and we could hang out for a while. We haven't gotten to do that much since you've been here."

"Oh, Trace, I'm sorry. I can't. Luke is working the morning shift so he can spend the afternoon here. I'll be with him, but it's sweet of you to ask. Maybe we can go for coffee or something next week when the Christmas rush is over."

He sighed. "Maybe so. Anyway, there's something else I wanted to talk with you about."

"All right. Let's go in the den and have a seat."

She'd no sooner said the words that she saw Maggie stick her head out from the dining room door and then jerk it back inside. Cheyenne smiled but didn't let on like she'd seen her. The little detective was on the prowl again trying to find out Christmas secrets.

She stopped at the den door and watched as Trace took off his coat and draped it over a chair before he walked to the sofa. "Have a seat, Trace. I need to check on something in the kitchen, but I'll be right back."

He slumped down on the couch. "No problem. Go ahead."

She turned and walked into the dining room, where she found Maggie plastered against the side of the wall. The little girl looked up when she entered. Cheyenne almost laughed out loud at the innocent expression Maggie directed at her. Her mouth pulled into the winning smile she always directed at someone when she was trying to get her way. Cheyenne tried to control her twitching lips as she stared down at the gap where Maggie had lost her two front teeth.

"Hi, Cheyenne," she murmured.

Cheyenne squatted down so that she was at eye level with her. "Hi, Maggie. Where's your mom and dad?"

"Mommy had to run to the grocery store, and I've been helping Daddy water the horses at the barn."

"Then why are you in the house?"

"He told me I could come get a snack. I was going back when I heard Luke leaving. I wanted to say 'bye to him, but that other man came before I could."

Cheyenne nodded. "I see. That other man is Trace. He and his father own the Wild West show. He's a friend of mine, and he's here to wish me a merry Christmas."

Maggie's eyes grew large. "Does he have a present for you?"

Cheyenne laughed. "I don't think so. I didn't see one in his hands."

Maggie tilted her head to one side. "Maybe it's small, and he has it in his pocket."

"There's no present, Maggie. Now you need to go back to the barn with your dad. Trace wants to talk to me."

"About what?" Maggie asked.

"I don't know. Now scoot. I'll see you later."

Maggie stared at her for a moment, and then a mischievous grin crossed her face. "If he has one, can I help you open it?"

From the first day since she'd come to Little Pigeon Ranch she and Maggie had shared a special bond, and all the child could think about was that Christmas was tomorrow. She hoped Maggie never lost her love for the holiday. So she needed to be patient with a little girl who was filled with excitement.

She leaned closer to Maggie and patted her hand. "I promise I'll let you help me open all my presents, but right now I need to talk to

Trace. You need to go back to the barn before your dad starts worrying about you."

Maggie stared at her for a moment, then grinned and threw her arms around Cheyenne's neck. "I love you, Cheyenne. I'm glad you came to live with us."

"I am, too, and I love you." Cheyenne rose to her feet and watched as Maggie turned and ran from the dining room. She waited until she heard the back door slam before she went back into the den. Trace was still sitting on the couch where she'd left him, and he looked up as she walked into the room. His face didn't hold the friendly look he'd had minutes ago. Now he directed a somber stare at her, and an uneasy feeling rippled through her.

"Are you okay, Trace?"

He nodded. "I've been better. I've just had some tough decisions to make lately, and they've caused me a lot of anxiety."

She dropped down on the sofa beside him and reached for his hand. "I hope there aren't any problems at the show. I know it was never your desire to be a part of it, but your dad was so insistent. I'm sure he's very proud of how hard you've worked to make it a success."

He stared at her for a moment. "You know

me well. We've shared a lot of good times, haven't we?"

She smiled. "Yes. You've been my friend ever since I was in high school and you joined my father's rodeo team. And now you've given me a job at your show. I want you to know that I will be back at work as soon as Patches is ready."

He waved his hand in dismissal. "It doesn't matter."

His reply and the way it was spoken concerned her, and she leaned forward. "Trace, there's something wrong. Do you want to tell me what it is?"

He stared at her for a moment. "I always get this way at Christmas. I thought maybe this year I could spend some time with you, but I guess Luke Conrad got here first."

She released his hand and swiveled to face him. "I thought you knew Luke and I had been seeing each other. He's also a friend of Dean and Gwen's, so it's not unusual that he'd spend Christmas with us."

His gaze raked her face. "Yeah, I knew, but I didn't think it would get serious. I thought he was just protecting you from your stalker, but I guess things are different now. Virgil Adkins is in jail, and you're ready to get on with your life. You have a new man in your life, and the future looks rosy for you."

She tilted her head to one side. "I wouldn't say that exactly. I'm relieved that I finally know who my stalker was. He'd kept his identity hidden for three years. I feel like I'm finally free to explore it."

He didn't say anything for a moment, as if he was pondering what she had just said. "I think that's a good idea to explore your options," Trace said. "There may be a lot that you haven't even discovered yet, but they may be there if you'd just reach out and take them. Have you thought about what you want to do? Of course, Dad and I want you to stay here and work for us. You have a job as long as you want one, but I didn't know if you wanted to move on somewhere else. Or even if Luke factored into what you want."

She thought about the things that she and Luke had said to each other just minutes ago, and she knew she didn't want to leave. She couldn't. She had to continue the journey that she and Luke had begun and see where it led them.

"I'm not going anywhere, Trace. I like it

here, and I'm thankful I can keep my job with the show. I promise you I'll have Patches back up to par. It'll just take some time after he's recovered enough to continue training. I can't really know when that will be."

Trace nodded and smiled. "We understand, and we don't want to rush you. It's very important that you don't come back before he's ready. We wouldn't want him to injure himself again."

"You're very understanding. Although I will admit, I'm going to miss having a paycheck."

Trace sat up straighter and stared at her. "That's no problem. I can help you out with that."

She waved her hand in dismissal. "No, I couldn't let you do that. I have money from the sale of our ranch in Wyoming. I just meant not having a regular paycheck makes me feel restless. Even when I was on the circuit, I was getting paid. But really, there's no need to worry about me."

He reached over and clasped her hand in his and rubbed his thumb over her knuckles. "I can't help it. I do worry about you. I don't want you dipping into your savings from the ranch when I can help you out."

"That's very sweet of you, Trace, but I'll be okay."

His hand tightened on hers. "So you don't want to take money from me?"

She shook her head. "It's not like that. I don't want to take advantage of you. We've been friends for too long."

He was silent for a moment as he continued to stare at their fingers intertwined. Then he spoke softly. "Would you take money from Luke Conrad if he offered it to you?"

The question shocked her, and she tried to pull her hand away. He tightened his grip and directed a stormy look at her. "What does Luke have to do with anything?" she asked.

"Because," Trace hissed. "I don't like the fact that you've gotten so friendly with him. He's not the man for you, and you need to end your relationship with him."

Cheyenne's mouth dropped open and she stared in disbelief at Trace. "What are you talking about? What gives you the right to judge who I can and who I can't have in my life?"

An angry growl escaped his mouth, and he released her hand long enough to grab both of her arms. "I have the right because I'm the man you're supposed to have in your life."

The words shocked Cheyenne so much that her body went rigid. "Wh-what are you talking about?" she whispered.

He gritted his teeth and increased his hold on her. "I remember the first day I saw you. I'd just joined your father's college rodeo team, and you came by the arena where we were practicing. You were sixteen years old and still in high school, but I knew that day we were meant for each other. I knew you were too young to have a relationship with me, so I decided to wait until you were older before I would say anything."

Cheyenne swallowed the fear that rose in her throat. "Trace, I'm sorry. I never did anything to encourage you. I thought you were my friend."

"I was your friend, Cheyenne. The best one you ever had. I listened to all your problems about the boys you dated, and it tore me up inside. But I knew my time with you was coming. Just when I thought I'd tell you how I felt, you told me you were off to college and the rodeo team there. But it didn't end there. You made me wait again by going on the rodeo circuit with your parents after you graduated, and you never gave me or what I wanted a thought. I stepped aside and let you have everything you wanted because I loved you so much."

Cheyenne shook her head in protest at Trace's words. "Please, Trace. Don't say any more."

His features hardened, and he gave her a shake. "I've been in torment for years because of you, so you can listen to what I have to say." He looked down at his fingers grasping her arms and relaxed his hold a bit. "Then one night at the Calgary Stampede you told me how lonely you were and how you wished you could meet someone to love. You described the kind of man you wanted, and I knew that was the way I could win you, could make you see that the man you'd wanted had been there all the time."

She remembered that night at the rodeo and the conversation they'd had in a diner near the arena after the evening's competition. She had performed her trick riding, and Trace had competed in bronc riding. They'd eaten a late dinner together, and she'd enjoyed being with him.

"Trace, please don't say anything else. I'm

sorry I didn't recognize how you felt. I wouldn't hurt you for anything."

"But you did," he muttered. "For years you've hurt me, but I knew that night how I could win you."

She didn't like the sinister tone his voice had suddenly taken. "How could you do that?"

"I could make you fall in love with me by being that man you wanted."

She frowned. "I don't understand."

"I could be someone else, a man you were just getting to know. Then after you'd fallen in love with me, I'd tell you who I really was."

She frowned. "But how? How could you…"

He leaned forward and smiled. "I could be Jesse Tolliver, and Jesse would be all you'd ever wanted."

"What?" she shrieked. She twisted to try and escape his grip, but he held her tighter.

"I was the one who told that girl in Calgary about the chat room and how she ought to join and get you to check it out, too. Once you were there, it didn't take a genius to figure out your username. Patches, really? Couldn't you have been more imaginative?"

A sudden thought struck her. "After my parents were killed, you kept trying to get me to come here and work for your father. I thought you were being nice to me, and all the time you wanted me closer so you could terrify me."

His eyes narrowed. "I was so angry with you, but I couldn't quit thinking about you. One day I loved you and the next I loathed you. You controlled all my thoughts until I was afraid I'd go mad."

"So that's why you sabotaged my drag strap. You wanted to kill me that night."

A contrite expression crossed his face. "I did, but after it was over I was sorry." He reached out and cupped her chin in his hand. "I didn't really want to hurt you, not deep down. All I wanted was for you to notice me. But after you came here, you ignored me as if I didn't exist. All you could think about was training for your performance, and you ignored me. I couldn't stop loving you, so I decided I'd give you one more chance to love me. Do you remember what I did when you showed up for your first performance?"

Cheyenne remembered that night very well. She'd been distracted because of the messages she'd gotten from her stalker, and it had barely registered with her when Trace asked her to go with him to get something to eat after the show. "You asked me out."

He nodded. "Yes, and what did you do after I'd decided to give you another chance? You rejected me. I cut your drag strap to teach you a lesson."

The stone-cold look on his face and the fire in his eyes terrified Cheyenne. She jerked free of his hold and jumped to her feet. Before she could escape, he grabbed her with one of his arms around her waist and the other over her chest. "Let me go," she yelled.

"No!" he shouted. "You aren't going anywhere until I'm through." His arms squeezed her tighter until she could hardly breathe. "But you didn't give *me* one more chance even after all I'd done for you," he continued. "You turned to Luke Conrad, and I knew it was going to be like it was before."

Cheyenne tried to ignore the fear and think rationally about how she could escape. "All right," she said in a calm, but shaky, voice. "I'll listen to whatever you have to say. Why don't you calm down. We can sit back down and discuss this rationally. I have some questions I need to ask you. Maybe you can help me see what I've done wrong."

Her statement seemed to pacify him for a moment, and his body relaxed some. "Okay," he said as he led her back to the couch and eased her down. "What do you want to know?"

She took a deep breath. "You say you loved me and wanted me to fall in love with you when you were Jesse. You wanted me to see that you had all the qualities I'd always told you I wanted in a man. If that's right, then why did you turn against me and start terrorizing me?"

"Because you began to talk about a new guy you'd met, and I knew you were doing it again. You were going to make me wait. When you wouldn't listen to me, I decided if I couldn't have you, no one else could."

"So you started sending me scary messages and stalking me everywhere I went." A horrible thought struck her, and her eyebrows shot up as she recoiled from him. "You killed my parents." The words escaped in a gush of air.

He nodded. "I went to see them and told them how I felt. They said they couldn't do anything, that who you fell in love with was your own decision. Then your father figured out I was the one you were afraid of and threatened to call the police. I couldn't do anything else. I had to kill them."

Tears ran down her face. "My parents were good to you. How could you do that?"

He shrugged. "It had to be done."

Another thought struck her, and she sat up straight. "Clint Shelton? Did you kill him, too, and try to make it look like he was the one who'd murdered my parents?"

"Yes, I wanted you to feel safe so you would turn to me. But you didn't," he growled.

Cheyenne's mind was working in double time. She had to find a way to get out of here. At the moment all she could think of was that if she kept Trace talking long enough Dean might come in from the barn and rescue her.

"So what about Virgil Adkins? How did you work that out?"

Trace chuckled. "Virgil is guilty of a lot of things, but being a threat to you isn't one of them. After I fired him, I told him I'd give him his last wages out of the petty cash in my father's office. That was too much of a temptation to him. I waited and watched, and sure enough he took the bait by stealing the money. I knew the combination to his locker, so it wasn't difficult to plant your music box there with the stolen money. But even after Virgil was arrested, you didn't turn to me, and I realized you never were going to. So I came to a decision."

"What kind of decision?"

"I'd give you one more chance. That's why I came today, but you rejected me again. This time it was for Luke Conrad."

"Trace, please..." she whispered as he reached up and trailed his index finger down the side of her face.

"I've loved you so much, but now I have to end this thing between us. If we can't be together in life, then we can be in death."

Her body started quivering, and she tried to pull back from him. "What do you mean?" she whispered in a shaky voice.

"Do you remember me telling you that my grandmother was Cherokee?"

"Yes."

"She lived on the Cherokee reservation over in North Carolina. I used to visit her in the summers, and we would always hike up to Mingo Falls. It was my favorite thing to do. I think she chose that trail for me because it wasn't too difficult, and the trip to the falls was worth it. We'd sit up on the rocks and look down at the water a hundred and twenty feet below while we ate sandwiches. I've been back there many times. I've always wanted to take you there, to share the beauty of the place with you. The time has come for me to do that."

This was getting crazier by the minute. "Why do you want me to see the falls?"

He looked at her as if he didn't understand the question. "Because I'm not going to leave you here for Luke Conrad. You're coming with me to Mingo Falls so we can fulfill our destiny."

She struggled to keep from letting him know how terrified she was. "I'm sorry, Trace. I'm not going anywhere with you and you need to go." She spoke as gently as she could. Maybe she could convince him to leave, and then she would call the police.

He sighed and nodded. "I suppose I do," he said. He didn't say anything else as he turned away and walked to the chair where he'd left his coat. He picked it up as if to put it on, but then turned around and pulled a gun from the pocket.

Her eyes grew large at the pistol pointed at her. "Trace, what are you doing? Put that gun down before it goes off."

He shook his head. "I'm through letting you jerk me around and mess up my life. I've done too much for you, but you don't appreciate it. It's time I quit trying to make you love me. Get your coat. We're leaving."

She took a step toward him, her hand extended. "Trace, please. Think about what you're doing."

"I know what I'm doing." He closed his eyes for a moment and bit down on his lip. "We're going to Mingo Falls, and when we get there, we're going to die together. Our bodies will rest together forever in a place of beauty and peace."

She recoiled at his words, her heart pounding. "Trace," she whispered.

He took a step forward and glared at her. "I'm not going to let Luke Conrad have you, and I can't live without you. So this thing between us will end at a place that is special to me." He motioned toward the hall tree, where her coat hung. "Get your coat, and let's go."

Cheyenne wanted to run, but she knew he would shoot if she did. Going with him wasn't what she wanted, but it might be the only way she could get away from him. Swallowing her fear, she nodded, stepped to the hall tree and slipped into her coat.

He stuck the gun in her back as he opened the front door, and she walked onto the porch. He nudged her with the gun, and she moved down the steps to his truck. He opened the door, and she felt the pressure of the gun barrel pressing into her back. "Get in, and don't try to run. I'm a good shot, and I'll kill you before you've taken two steps."

She nodded and climbed in the truck. When he ran around to get in on the driver's side, she reached for the door handle. This might be the only chance she had. Before she could act on the impulse, he was standing at the open door opposite her. "Try it and you won't live to tell about it."

She released her hold and folded her hands in her lap. Then he was in the truck, and they were roaring toward the road that ran in front of the ranch. She looked over her shoulder before they pulled onto the pavement and stared at the house she'd come to love. She hoped this wasn't the last time she would see it. She closed her eyes and breathed a prayer that somehow she could find a way to escape.

* * *

Luke glanced at the elf suit that lay on the truck seat beside him and wondered how Ben had talked him into putting that thing on and going to the hospital. With a sigh he shook his head. It was all for the benefit of the children who wouldn't be home for Christmas, and a little self-consciousness on his part wasn't too much to bear if it brought some cheer to them.

He smiled when he thought of the way Cheyenne had laughed when he told her what he was going to do. When she'd told him what a wonderful thing he was doing, though, he felt as if he could do anything in the world if it would make her proud of him. He'd waited a long time to find someone he thought he could love, and now he'd found her. Tomorrow they would spend Christmas together, and he only hoped it would be the first of many to come.

He hadn't shown her his home yet, and he looked forward to that. His father had loved horses, and Luke had kept the barn and corral in tip-top shape ever since his father died. It was a small tribute to him, and he hoped his dad would have approved. If things went well for Cheyenne and him, they might be sharing that home together in the future. The thought filled him with a warm feeling, and he smiled.

His ringing cell phone jerked him from his thoughts, and he glanced at the screen on his truck's dash. He'd been glad to see that this vehicle had Bluetooth capacity, and he could sync his phone to it.

The number displayed was from the sheriff's office, and he punched the screen to connect the call. "Conrad here," he said.

"Luke, this is Andy at the station."

"Hey, Andy. I didn't know you were working on Christmas Eve."

Andy chuckled. "Yeah, my work never ends."

"I'm on my way to the hospital to give out gifts to the children. What can I do for you?"

"You remember you had me tracing some emails off a computer a few weeks ago?"

Luke sat up straighter at Andy's question and looked around to find a place to pull over. If this was about Cheyenne, he needed to stop the truck and concentrate. He spotted a discount clothing store to his right, and he pulled into the parking lot and came to a stop.

"Yeah. I remember. What about it?"

"Well, I've continued to monitor those ISPs we found, especially the ones around here, to see if that computer shows up again, and today it worked out."

Luke's breath froze in his throat. "How?"

"I figured he'd finally slip up, and he did. Do you remember I told you that there's no way to tell who owns a computer when they log in on a public ISP. On the other hand the computer has a unique identity that registers, and I could see every time that same computer logged in at the same public internet provider."

"Yeah, I remember. You also told me that the only way you could identify the owner was if that computer logged in to a personal account like an online bank account or a credit card from that same location."

"Well, he finally did it. He logged in today at a fast-food restaurant next to where the Wild West show is. He'd used that one before when he was sending emails to Cheyenne, but this time he went to his bank account."

"His bank account? That means you know his name."

"Yep, I sure do. It's Trace Johnson."

For a moment Luke could only sit in stunned silence. "Trace Johnson? Are you sure about that, Andy?"

"I'm positive. The same computer that sent

those emails went to Trace Johnson's online bank account about an hour ago."

Luke groaned and pounded the steering wheel. "Oh, no!"

"What's the matter, Luke?"

"That means he's the one who's been stalking her and I just left them together. I've got to call her."

Before Andy could reply, he'd disconnected the call and had looked up Cheyenne's number. It rang several times before it went to voice mail. "Cheyenne, where are you?" he muttered under his breath.

Maybe she was at the barn and had left her cell phone in the house. His heart pounded in his chest as he tried Dean's number. He answered on the first ring. "Hello."

"Dean, it's Luke. Is Cheyenne there with you?"

"No, I think she's up at the house. Try her there."

"She's not answering her phone, and I need to talk to her. I just found out…"

Before he could finish, he heard Maggie's voice screaming in the background. "Daddy! Daddy! A bad man took Cheyenne!"

His blood felt as if it had turned to ice, and his body jerked. "Dean! What is Maggie saying?"

"I don't know. Hold on."

"Daddy!" the child cried again and then the sound was muffled.

He could hear Dean trying to calm her as he spoke softly. "Baby, tell me what's wrong. What about Cheyenne?"

"Her friend, that man from the Wild West show, came to see her. He took her away." Maggie wailed, and Luke thought for a moment his heart had stopped beating.

"Maggie," Dean said, "tell me what happened, sweetheart. How do you know this?"

"I thought he had her a Christmas present, and I wanted to see. So I tiptoed in the dining room to listen to them, but I got scared because he was yelling at Cheyenne."

"What did he say?"

"He said she was going with him. She didn't want to go, but he made her. I peeked out at them when they got to the front door, and he had a gun." Maggie's last word ended with a wail.

Luke's chest suddenly squeezed, and he thought he was going to pass out. He closed his eyes and took a deep breath. "Luke!" Dean's voice came over the phone. "Did you hear that?"

"I did," Luke answered. "Ask Maggie if she has any idea where they were going."

Dean asked the question, but Luke couldn't hear the answer. Finally Dean spoke again. "She doesn't know, but she did hear him say something about a waterfall and his grandmother."

"Thanks, Dean. I've got to go. I'll be in touch."

He didn't give Dean time to say anything else before he was calling the sheriff's office. Clara answered right away. "Sheriff's office."

"Clara, this is Luke. Trace Johnson has kidnapped Cheyenne Cassidy. I need a BOLO put out on him right away. Tell the officers he's armed and dangerous."

"You got it, Luke."

"And call me if there are any sightings."

"I will."

He disconnected the call and sat there for a moment. "Think," he muttered out loud as he pounded the steering wheel. "Where do I turn now?"

An idea popped into his head and he made another phone call. Bill Johnson answered right away. "Hello."

"Bill, this is Luke. I need to find Trace. Do

you know of a waterfall that has some connection to his grandmother?"

"Yeah. It's Mingo Falls over close to Cherokee. He used to go there all the time with her."

A small hope washed over him. "I know the place. Thanks, Bill."

"Luke, what's this about?"

But he had no time to answer. He'd already disconnected that call and was placing another one. Clara answered. "Luke? Do you have something?"

"He's going to Mingo Falls. My guess is he'll go on Highway 441 since that's a direct route to Cherokee. I'm on my way. Let the others know."

He'd barely gone a mile when his cell phone rang and he connected. It was Clara. "Luke, Patterson spotted him. He's on 441 headed into the park."

Luke frowned. "Then we need to stop him before he crosses the state line at Newfound Gap and leaves our jurisdiction. Call the sheriff over in Cherokee County and ask him to set up a roadblock so he can't get past there. Maybe we can stop him at the gap."

"Got it," Clara said as she disconnected.

Luke pressed down on the accelerator, and

his truck lurched forward. As he raced along the road, all he could think about was how scared Cheyenne must be, and he prayed over and over. "Don't let him hurt her, God. Please don't let him hurt her."

FOURTEEN

Cheyenne kept hoping that Trace would put the gun down, but he'd kept it on his knees with his left hand on it ever since they'd left the ranch. From time to time his fingers wrapped around the trigger, and she held her breath expecting him to shoot at any moment.

They hadn't talked since they'd gotten in the truck, and she was afraid that anything she said might set him off. So she'd chosen to be quiet and try to figure out a way that she could escape from him. Nothing had come to her yet.

It had been clear to her from the time he forced her into the vehicle that there was no help for her. No one knew where she was and what had happened. They probably wouldn't miss her for hours, and then it would be too late. She would probably be dead at the bottom of Mingo Falls. The thought sent fear racing through her, and she closed her eyes.

She turned her head and stared out the window as he drove farther along the national park road that crossed the mountains from Tennessee to North Carolina. She'd intended to take this drive ever since she moved here, but she never had. Now she was being transported across the mountains by a psychopath who intended to kill her.

For a moment her thoughts went to Luke. She'd hoped there might be a happily-ever-after for them, but it looked doubtful now. Her life was going to end soon unless she did something.

She spotted a road sign displaying a distance of four miles to Newfound Gap, the lowest point on the ridge through the mountains. She also knew the North Carolina line was there. In a few minutes she'd be in another state.

"No!" Trace suddenly shouted, and she straightened in her seat.

"What's wrong?"

"I can see a police car behind us."

She twisted in the seat to look through the rear window and felt a ray of hope at the sight of a squad car in the distance, its blue lights flashing, bearing down on them. Before she could say anything, Trace pressed the accelerator to the floor and they skidded around a sharp curve. Cheyenne braced for the crash she felt was about to come as the truck hit the shoulder of the road and raced along the side of the mountain.

She stared out the window at the drop-off of the mountain hillside to her right. The truck dislodged some rocks at the edge of the road, and they tumbled downward in a small rock slide before Trace regained control of the vehicle. He muttered under his breath as the truck surged forward, snapping her neck back.

They sped along for a few miles with her gripping the edge of her seat and Trace trying to keep control of the speeding truck. She knew that Newfound Gap lay just ahead, and she wondered if the sheriff's car would pursue them into North Carolina. Probably not.

Suddenly Trace slammed on the brakes, and the car skidded to a stop. If she hadn't been wearing her seat belt, she was sure she would have gone through the windshield. She stared straight ahead. Her heart jumped into her throat at the sight of North Carolina police officers blocking the road just over the state line. Behind them, she could hear the sirens of the approaching Tennessee officers.

Trace gunned the accelerator again and roared into the parking lot of the overlook at Newfound Gap. The truck came to an abrupt stop, and he was out of it before she could get her seat belt unfastened.

This was her chance to escape. She reached for the door handle, but before she even touched it, he had jerked open the door. He had the gun aimed at her and a furious look on his face. "Get out! Now!" he bellowed.

She scrambled from the car and he grabbed her by the arm. Behind them she heard the police cars coming to a halt in the parking lot, but Trace tightened his hold on her and dragged her forward along the north side of the parking area toward the Rockefeller Memorial, where President Franklin Roosevelt had officially dedicated the Smoky Mountain National Park years ago. She'd never been here, but she'd seen pictures of the semicircular stone structure elevated above the ground with a clump of trees behind it.

The gray stone structure reminded her of a fortress tucked into the mountainside. She swallowed the bile that rose in her throat as she spotted the winding steps that led to the top. They provided the only ascent, and a sudden thought filled her with fear. That memorial was like an impenetrable fort towering over the parking lot. If Trace forced her to the top, he would probably kill them both before anyone could reach them.

As Trace pulled her forward, she stumbled, but he jerked her to her feet. "What are you doing?" she shouted. "You need to give yourself up."

He looked at her and snarled. "I guess we won't make it to Mingo Falls. It looks like we'll die here, and the top of the memorial is as good a place as any."

She swallowed her fear as he forced her to the side of the structure and up the steps to the very top. They emerged onto the flat surface, where thousands of visitors came each year to get a good view of the mountains around.

There were no people in the parking lot or at the memorial today probably because it was Christmas Eve. She was glad. At least no innocent people would be caught in this situation.

Trace pushed her to the floor and sank down beside her. They sat with their backs to the wall as they heard more cars come to a stop in the parking lot. Then she heard a voice calling out. "Trace, make it easy on yourself. Let her go."

Her heart began to pound, and she breathed a sigh of relief. Luke was here. He'd found her, and he was going to save her. Her joy was short-lived, however, when she glanced at Trace and saw the rage on his face. "So he came after you. Too bad he's not going to be able to save you."

Suddenly he grabbed her arm, jerked her to her feet and pushed her against the waist-high wall facing the parking lot. He stood behind her with his arm around her and his gun pointed at her head.

As she looked out over the parking lot, she could see sheriff's deputies as well as some highway patrol officers and North Carolina officers in the parking lot. Some were crouched beside their cars, and others peered around the backs of theirs. Then she saw Luke. He stood beside his truck and stared up at her. He raised a bullhorn to his mouth and spoke into it.

"Let Cheyenne go, Trace. We don't want anybody to get hurt here today."

"Back off, Conrad," Trace yelled back. "I'll shoot any man who comes closer, but I'll reserve the last two bullets. One for her and one for me. If you make one move toward me, I'll kill her."

"You don't want to do that. There's no escape for you. Make it easy on yourself and let her go."

Trace became more agitated and he pressed the gun tighter to her head. "We're going to escape this world together. We're going to die right here."

"Nobody has to die today, Trace. Put the gun down and give yourself up. It'll go better for you if you do."

"I know what you're doing, Conrad!" Trace shouted. "You want to save Cheyenne for yourself, but I'm not going to let you have her. Now back off before I kill her right now."

He aimed the gun and fired two shots at Luke. Cheyenne screamed as they both kicked up dust just inches away from Luke. Then Trace yanked her back down to the floor of the memorial and pressed her against the wall. "Don't move," he threatened.

She was too scared to answer, so she just nodded. He slid to the floor beside her and leaned back against the wall. She watched as he closed his eyes and raked his hand through his hair. She had no idea how long they sat like that, her staring at him as he became more agitated. From time to time she heard a groan, and he would press his finger to the trigger. Every time he did, her heart exploded with fear.

Then he began to mutter. "When it gets dark. When it gets dark."

It dawned on her what he'd been trying to do for the last few minutes. He'd been trying to get up enough courage to end their lives, and she knew what he'd decided. They were both going to die when it got dark, and from the looks of the lengthening shadows, that time wasn't far off.

Luke felt helpless. Cheyenne was at the top of the memorial with a killer, and any move on their part could put her life at risk. He stood beside his truck and kept his eyes trained on the spot where he'd seen her earlier. Now that night was falling, he could make out the shape of the memorial, but he hadn't seen her again. He could only imagine how terrified she must be.

He heard footsteps approaching behind, and he turned to see Ben striding forward. He came to a stop next to Luke. "Any changes?"

"No. We've got to do something, Ben. The temperature's beginning to drop. I can't stand to think about Cheyenne up there hungry and cold with a gun pointed to her head."

"I've been discussing our options with the tactical team that's come in. They're trying to figure out the best strategy. If we storm the place, we run the risk of him shooting her. Do you have a suggestion?"

Luke exhaled a deep breath. "Yeah. I think one man might have a chance to get up those stairs in the dark and take him by surprise."

Ben looked at him. "That sounds risky and dangerous. Who are you suggesting for the job?"

"Me. I've climbed those stairs dozens of times in the past. In the dark I can go down the south side of the parking lot and circle around until I can get to the base of the steps. Then I can slip up the steps to the top and take him down."

Ben looked at him with a skeptical look on his face. "Just like that you're going to take him down. Luke, he'll shoot you before you set foot on the top of the memorial."

Luke shook his head. "Not if I'm careful. I

carried out at least a dozen missions like this when I was in the army. I can do it."

Ben studied his face for a moment and then sighed. "Are you sure? It might—"

"I have to try," Luke interrupted. "I love her, Ben."

Ben studied him a moment before he finally sighed and nodded. "Okay. What can we do to help?"

"While I'm working my way around, you keep talking to him. Ask him to let you see Cheyenne again. Just say anything to keep him distracted and give me time."

Ben nodded. "Okay. But be careful."

Luke nodded and slipped into the shadows down the south side of the parking lot. As he made his way down the slope, he could hear Ben's voice echoing in the night. "Hey, Johnson. I want to talk to you."

For a few minutes there was no sound, then Trace answered. "What about?"

"It's getting cold out here. I don't know what kind of coat you have, but you've lived in these mountains long enough to know December nights can be rough, and it's even more so at this elevation."

"So?"

"So, I just want to help you out. I thought you and Cheyenne might need some blankets or some hot food. How about that?"

"You can't fool me. You don't want to help me. You'll promise anything if you think I'll let you have Cheyenne," Trace yelled.

"I want to help both of you. We've got lots of men out here, and they aren't going anywhere. All of us are cold and getting hungry. You can end all this if you just come on down, and we'll get you warm and get some hot food in you."

"I know that's you, Ben, and you can save your breath. The only way we're leaving the top of this memorial is in body bags."

As Ben continued to coax Trace to give himself up, Luke kept moving until he had worked himself around to the side of the structure, where a steep flight of steps led to the top. The ground crunched under his feet, and he stilled to make sure he hadn't been heard. He could tell he was standing on some rocks, and he reached down and put two in his pocket.

"Trace," Ben called out, "how is Cheyenne doing?"

"Don't worry about her. She's fine."

"It sure would make me feel better to see

for myself. Why don't you let her stand up and show me?"

Luke pulled his gun from his holster and gripped it with both hands in front of him. He put his foot onto the first step and eased up to the second.

"I tell you she's fine," Trace yelled.

"Just let me see for myself. That's all I'm asking."

As silently as he could, Luke moved up the steps until he was standing with his back against the wall in the curve that led to the top. All he had to do was take that last step onto the landing, and he would be face-to-face with Cheyenne's captor. He said a quick prayer for a steady hand and a safe rescue.

"Let me see her, Trace," Ben called.

Luke heard a rustling noise and a protesting grunt from Cheyenne as she was pulled to her feet. "Here she is, Ben," Trace yelled. "Are you satisfied?"

Luke peered around the corner and caught sight of Trace standing behind Cheyenne with his body pressed against her as he held her to the wall facing the parking lot. Luke reached in his pocket and threw one of the rocks against the far end of the memorial. It struck the side, and the sound echoed in the night.

Surprised, Trace whirled around with his weapon pointed in that direction and fired. His hand that still held Cheyenne loosened, and she jerked free of his grip. Luke took a leap onto the floor of the memorial. "Drop the gun, Trace," he shouted.

Trace froze for a moment, and then he whirled with the gun pointed at Luke. Before he could fire his gun, Luke pulled the trigger and Trace dropped to the ground. Luke rushed forward and kicked the gun away before he turned to Cheyenne.

She had sunk to the floor and sat huddled against the wall, her body shaking. He knelt beside her and touched her face. "Cheyenne, are you all right?"

She looked up at him, and even in the dark he could see the tears in her eyes. "You came for me," she whispered.

He stroked her hair and smiled at her. "I always will, darling. I always will."

With a little cry she fell against him as her tears began to fall, and he put his arms around her. Behind him the sound of boots pounding on the steps could be heard, and Ben and the other officers appeared as they reached the top of the memorial. Luke sat with his back against the wall and cradled Cheyenne in his arms.

He heard Ben on his cell phone calling for an ambulance, and he looked up at him. "How's Trace?"

"He's alive. We'll get him to the hospital. That was good work, Luke." He looked down at Cheyenne, who was nestled against him, and smiled. "It looks like it turned out good all the way around. Merry Christmas."

"And merry Christmas to you, too," Luke said as he hugged Cheyenne tighter and kissed the top of her head.

He closed his eyes and sat still for a moment as the events of the past few hours replayed in his mind. For a while there he thought his chance at happiness might be coming to an end, but God had watched over them. For the first time in three years Cheyenne was safe. Now they could face the future together.

Tomorrow really was going to be the best Christmas he'd ever had.

Cheyenne sat in the den with Maggie looking at the pile of presents she'd unwrapped earlier. She'd never seen anyone so excited, and she'd enjoyed watching the child's eyes light up more as she opened one after another.

She thought back over the day so far, and a warm glow settled over her. They'd started with just the four of them—Dean, Gwen, Maggie and her—coming downstairs to open presents, then indulged in a big breakfast in the kitchen.

Dean had chosen this year not to book any guests at the ranch over the holidays. He wanted the house to themselves and didn't want to be distracted by having to take care of visitors. He had even given all the employees the day off to enjoy the holiday. It had really been a day for family, and Cheyenne realized how fortunate she was to have this one she now called her own.

Tantalizing smells drifted from the kitchen, and her stomach growled in anticipation of what Gwen was cooking for the dinner they would have midafternoon. She couldn't wait for that, but what she was looking forward to most was Luke's arrival.

"Cheyenne," Maggie said, interrupting her thoughts. "I'm glad that man didn't hurt you yesterday."

Cheyenne reached over and kissed Maggie

on the cheek. "Thanks to you I was rescued. I think you were really the heroine yesterday. If it wasn't for you, no one would have known what happened to me."

Maggie looked down at the floor. "Yeah, but I didn't obey you. I came back in the house after you told me to go to the barn."

Cheyenne laughed and put her arm around Maggie's shoulders. "I think we can overlook that this time. Everything turned out the way it was supposed to."

"I guess so," Maggie said. Then she looked down at the new doll and all its clothes that she'd gotten for Christmas. "Want to help me dress Sally for Christmas dinner?"

"I'd love to," she answered.

Twenty minutes later they were sitting on the floor, doll clothes all around, and discussing which outfit would look best at dinner, when a knock sounded at the door. "I'll get it," Maggie said as she jumped up.

Cheyenne heard the door open, and then she heard his voice. "Maggie, how's my girl doing today? Did you get a lot of presents?"

"Oh, Luke," Maggie squealed. "Wait until you see everything I got."

Cheyenne smiled as they appeared in the

door, Maggie pulling Luke after her. His eyes warmed when he saw her and he came to a stop next to her. "How are you feeling?" he asked.

"I'm fine. We're dressing Maggie's doll for dinner. Want to help?"

"I can't think of anything I'd like better," he said as he plopped down on the floor next to her.

They were still sitting there thirty minutes later when Gwen appeared at the door. "Maggie, it may be Christmas, but you still have your chores to do. Go on and get them over with before dinner."

Maggie nodded and jumped to her feet. "I have to feed and water my dog and my pony. I won't be gone long."

With that she ran from the room. Gwen watched her leave, then smiled at them. "I'll try to keep her occupied for a while so you two can have some time together."

Cheyenne felt her face grow warm. "You don't have to do that, Gwen."

Gwen arched an eyebrow. "Oh, I think I do." Her gaze lit on Luke, and a somber expression crossed her face. "I want to thank you for what you did for Cheyenne yesterday. That was very brave of you, and we appreciate it."

He looked at Cheyenne and smiled. "It was my pleasure."

"I understand Trace Johnson is going to live," she added.

Luke nodded. "Yeah, he'll stand trial for stalking, for attempted murder and kidnapping here. Of course, there are charges against him in Wyoming for the murder of Cheyenne's parents and Clint Shelton. I don't think he'll ever see the light of day outside a prison again."

Cheyenne glanced up at him. "Have you talked to Bill?"

"I have."

"How's he taking it?"

Luke sighed. "Not so good, I'm afraid. It seems like he's always been hard on Trace. Now he wishes he could go back and do things differently to try and help him. Of course, it's too late for that."

"I feel so sorry for him," Cheyenne said.

Gwen took a deep breath. "Let's not talk any more about the bad things that happened. This is Christmas, and we need to celebrate. I'll call you when dinner's ready."

"Need any help?" Cheyenne called after her as she walked away.

"I've got it under control. Enjoy being with Luke."

Cheyenne turned back to Luke, and he was smiling. He leaned over and brushed his lips across hers. "I think we're being set up again."

She grinned. "I think so, too. Are you sorry?"

He reached up and tucked a stray lock of hair behind her ear. "Not a bit. I'm so thankful everything turned out as it did. I feel like we've been given a great gift, and I want to enjoy just being with you."

"I want that, too," she whispered as he put his arm around her and drew her close. She laid her head on his shoulder. "You really are one of a kind, Luke Conrad."

He smiled. "How so?"

She snuggled closer. "Well, for starters you carry a gun in your job, and you're the bravest man I've ever known. Even so, you're not afraid to dress up like an elf to brighten the day for children in the hospital. You don't mind sitting on the floor and helping a little girl dress her dolls. And besides all that, you still took time to save my life again."

He turned his head to stare down at her. "Again? When did I do it before?"

She twisted in his arms until she was facing him. Then she slipped her arms around his neck and looked up into the blue eyes that had almost taken her breath away the day she'd run in front of his car. "When you taught me how I could learn to live with myself and overcome my guilt. That changed my life and saved me from the prison I'd put myself in, Luke. I'll always be grateful to you for that."

He smiled. "And here I thought I was the one who should be grateful. I've been lonely for so many years, and I wanted someone to share my life with. I'd almost given up hope. Then you came along, and I knew my life would never be the same again."

He lowered his head until his lips were only inches from hers. "Merry Christmas, Cheyenne Cassidy. I love you."

"Merry Christmas, Luke Conrad. I love you, too."

His lips pressed down on hers, and she didn't think about Trace Johnson or anything that had happened to her in the past few years.

Luke had helped her put that behind her. Now she had a future to look forward to, and it included the man she loved.

EPILOGUE

Six months later

Cheyenne stood beside Patches backstage at the Wild West show and waited for their time to perform. Right now there was a drill team of horses in the arena, and the crowd was going wild. She only hoped they felt the same when she did her act.

This was her first performance back, and she was scared. She'd told herself a dozen times that she had nothing to worry about. Patches had been released by the vet, and he was as good as new. They'd picked up their training just where they'd left off, but she still couldn't help being a little nervous.

"Are you ready?" a voice behind her asked.

She turned and smiled as Luke walked up and stopped beside her. "What are you doing back here? I thought you were going to sit with Dean and Gwen."

"I have been. I've even eaten some of Maggie's cotton candy, but I wanted to come and see you before you perform. This is a big night for you. It's been nearly seven months since you performed, and I know you're apprehensive."

She nodded. "I think the nerves are normal. I just want to do my best."

"I don't have any doubt that you will." He looked around. "Have you seen Ken yet?"

"I saw him at a distance, but I haven't talked to him."

"How's he making out?"

Cheyenne shrugged. "I think he's doing okay. He'd always wanted to own a show like this, and he snapped it up the minute Bill put it up for sale. I was sorry to see Bill leave, but I understood his reasons for not wanting to stay here."

Luke sighed. "Let's just hope he can find some peace in his life." He reached down, pulled her left hand to his lips and kissed the diamond ring he'd given to her a week ago. "You've sure brought some to me."

"As you have for me," she said. "I can't believe we're getting married this summer."

"Well, we are." He hesitated a moment and a troubled look played across his face. "You do like my ranch, don't you?"

She threw back her head and laughed. "How many times do I have to assure you that I love it? The house is perfect, and the barn is wonderful. And I also like the idea of our starting a business that I can operate while you're off chasing law breakers. I've always wanted to have my own place, where I could have a riding stable that also boards other people's horses and train the ones we're raising for sale. Maybe in a few years we can even get into horse breeding."

He smiled. "You have it all figured out, don't you?"

"No, I think we'll have some problems along the way. Every business does, but we've got one thing on our side. We love each other, and we want a future together."

He stared down for a moment before he smiled. "You got that right, lady." Then he brushed his lips across hers. "Now go out there and show everybody what you can do."

"I will," she whispered.

She watched as he turned and walked away. Ken Dandridge, the new owner, ran up to her and stopped. "Cheyenne, you're on next. Everything all right?"

"Everything's fine, Ken," she said as she swung into the saddle and stood up in preparation for the hippodrome stand, the trick she always performed as she entered the arena. She closed her eyes for a moment and wished that her parents were here, but she knew if they were they would be happy for her. They would like Luke, and they'd want them to have a happy life together.

She could hear the announcer as he began his introduction, and she smiled. "And now, ladies and gentlemen," he declared in a booming voice, "get ready for the thrill of a lifetime as after a seven-month absence, the Smoky Mountain Wild West Show welcomes back Cheyenne Cassidy, three-time women's International Trick Riding Competition award winner. Put your hands together and give a Smoky Mountain cheer for Cheyenne and her horse, Patches!"

The door opened, and Patches galloped into the arena with Cheyenne perched in a standing position on the saddle. Applause and whistles rang out as they sped around the ring. Somewhere in the crowd she knew that Luke was watching, and he was cheering. She closed her eyes and basked in the moment as Patches galloped around the ring, while Cheyenne's body stood straight and balanced on the saddle as her hair blew backward.

She'd missed performing, and now she was back. But this time it was so much better. There was no stalker, no one to make her life miserable. Instead she had found a man who made every day seem like a new adventure, and she was going to spend the rest of her life living it.

* * * * *

Be sure to pick up the first story in
SMOKY MOUNTAIN SECRETS:

IN A KILLER'S SIGHTS

Find more great reads at
www.LoveInspired.com.

Dear Reader,

I hope you enjoyed *Stalking Season*, the second book in my Smoky Mountain Secrets series. As I researched and wrote this book, I developed a deep heartache for the victims who endure the nightmare of being stalked. Not only did Cheyenne have to endure the fear of being watched, she also had to contend with guilt that her actions had brought about the deaths of her parents. She came to know, however, that just as God forgives the choices we make, we can learn to forgive ourselves. It is God's intention that His children should live in peace. If you haven't come to know the comfort He can bring to your life, I pray that you will seek what He offers.

Sandra Robbins

LARGER-PRINT BOOKS!

GET 2 FREE LARGER-PRINT NOVELS PLUS 2 FREE MYSTERY GIFTS

Love Inspired®

Larger-print novels are now available...

YES! Please send me 2 FREE LARGER-PRINT Love Inspired® novels and my 2 FREE mystery gifts (gifts are worth about $10). After receiving them, if I don't wish to receive any more books, I can return the shipping statement marked "cancel." If I don't cancel, I will receive 6 brand-new novels every month and be billed just $5.49 per book in the U.S. or $5.99 per book in Canada. That's a savings of at least 19% off the cover price. It's quite a bargain! Shipping and handling is just 50¢ per book in the U.S. and 75¢ per book in Canada.* I understand that accepting the 2 free books and gifts places me under no obligation to buy anything. I can always return a shipment and cancel at any time. Even if I never buy another book, the two free books and gifts are mine to keep forever.

122/322 IDN GH6D

Name	(PLEASE PRINT)
Address	Apt. #
City	State/Prov.	Zip/Postal Code

Signature (if under 18, a parent or guardian must sign)

Mail to the **Reader Service**:
IN U.S.A.: P.O. Box 1867, Buffalo, NY 14240-1867
IN CANADA: P.O. Box 609, Fort Erie, Ontario L2A 5X3

Are you a current subscriber to Love Inspired® books and want to receive the larger-print edition?
Call 1-800-873-8635 or visit www.ReaderService.com.

* Terms and prices subject to change without notice. Prices do not include applicable taxes. Sales tax applicable in N.Y. Canadian residents will be charged applicable taxes. Offer not valid in Quebec. This offer is limited to one order per household. Not valid to current subscribers to Love Inspired Larger-Print books. All orders subject to credit approval. Credit or debit balances in a customer's account(s) may be offset by any other outstanding balance owed by or to the customer. Please allow 4 to 6 weeks for delivery. Offer available while quantities last.

Your Privacy—The Reader Service is committed to protecting your privacy. Our Privacy Policy is available online at www.ReaderService.com or upon request from the Reader Service.

We make a portion of our mailing list available to reputable third parties that offer products we believe may interest you. If you prefer that we not exchange your name with third parties, or if you wish to clarify or modify your communication preferences, please visit us at www.ReaderService.com/consumerschoice or write to us at Reader Service Preference Service, P.O. Box 9062, Buffalo, NY 14240-9062. Include your complete name and address.

LILP15

REQUEST YOUR FREE BOOKS!
2 FREE WHOLESOME ROMANCE NOVELS IN LARGER PRINT
PLUS 2
FREE
MYSTERY GIFTS

🌸🌸🌸🌸🌸🌸🌸🌸🌸🌸🌸🌸🌸🌸🌸🌸🌸

HEARTWARMING™
🌸🌸🌸🌸🌸🌸🌸🌸🌸🌸🌸🌸🌸🌸🌸🌸🌸🌸🌸🌸

Wholesome, tender romances

YES! Please send me 2 FREE Harlequin® Heartwarming Larger-Print novels and my 2 FREE mystery gifts (gifts worth about $10). After receiving them, if I don't wish to receive any more books, I can return the shipping statement marked "cancel." If I don't cancel, I will receive 4 brand-new larger-print novels every month and be billed just $5.24 per book in the U.S. or $5.99 per book in Canada. That's a savings of at least 19% off the cover price. It's quite a bargain! Shipping and handling is just 50¢ per book in the U.S. and 75¢ per book in Canada.* I understand that accepting the 2 free books and gifts places me under no obligation to buy anything. I can always return a shipment and cancel at any time. Even if I never buy another book, the two free books and gifts are mine to keep forever.

161/361 IDN GHX2

Name _____ (PLEASE PRINT) _____

Address _____ Apt. # _____

City _____ State/Prov. _____ Zip/Postal Code _____

Signature (if under 18, a parent or guardian must sign)

Mail to the **Reader Service:**
IN U.S.A.: P.O. Box 1867, Buffalo, NY 14240-1867
IN CANADA: P.O. Box 609, Fort Erie, Ontario L2A 5X3

* Terms and prices subject to change without notice. Prices do not include applicable taxes. Sales tax applicable in N.Y. Canadian residents will be charged applicable taxes. Offer not valid in Quebec. This offer is limited to one order per household. Not valid for current subscribers to Harlequin Heartwarming larger-print books. All orders subject to credit approval. Credit or debit balances in a customer's account(s) may be offset by any other outstanding balance owed by or to the customer. Please allow 4 to 6 weeks for delivery. Offer available while quantities last.

Your Privacy—The Reader Service is committed to protecting your privacy. Our Privacy Policy is available online at www.ReaderService.com or upon request from the Reader Service.

We make a portion of our mailing list available to reputable third parties that offer products we believe may interest you. If you prefer that we not exchange your name with third parties, or if you wish to clarify or modify your communication preferences, please visit us at www.ReaderService.com/consumerschoice or write to us at Reader Service Preference Service, P.O. Box 9062, Buffalo, NY 14240-9062. Include your complete name and address.

HW15

YES! Please send me **The Western Promises Collection** in Larger Print. This collection begins with 3 FREE books and 2 FREE gifts (gifts valued at approx. $14.00 retail) in the first shipment, along with the other first 4 books from the collection! If I do not cancel, I will receive 8 monthly shipments until I have the entire 51-book Western Promises collection. I will receive 2 or 3 FREE books in each shipment and I will pay just $4.99 US/ $5.89 CDN for each of the other four books in each shipment, plus $2.99 for shipping and handling per shipment. *If I decide to keep the entire collection, I'll have paid for only 32 books, because 19 books are FREE! I understand that accepting the 3 free books and gifts places me under no obligation to buy anything. I can always return a shipment and cancel at any time. My free books and gifts are mine to keep no matter what I decide.

272 HCN 3070 472 HCN 3070

Name _____ (PLEASE PRINT) _____

Address _____ Apt. # _____

City _____ State/Prov. _____ Zip/Postal Code _____

Signature (if under 18, a parent or guardian must sign) _____

Mail to the **Reader Service:**
IN U.S.A.: P.O. Box 1867, Buffalo, NY 14240-1867
IN CANADA: P.O. Box 609, Fort Erie, Ontario L2A 5X3

READERSERVICE.COM

Manage your account online!

- Review your order history
- Manage your payments
- Update your address

> *We've designed the*
> *Reader Service website*
> *just for you.*

Enjoy all the features!

- Discover new series available to you, and read excerpts from any series.
- Respond to mailings and special monthly offers.
- Connect with favorite authors at the blog.
- Browse the Bonus Bucks catalog and online-only exculsives.
- Share your feedback.

Visit us at:

ReaderService.com